T0352134

PRAISE FOR HAMLET AND THE PSYCHOTHERAPIST

"When a team of 21st Century psychotherapists travel back to Elizabethan London, they treat a melancholy young prince named Hamlet. Will their intervention change the action of the play or even the course of theatrical history? In this witty and imaginative novel, Michael Kerr Scott creates a light-hearted, engaging, and remarkably authentic portrait of Shakespeare's London where theatre and daily life transform one another in unexpected ways. As they help Hamlet work through his own doubts and hesitations, the therapists discover that Shakespeare's theatre can illuminate and give meaning to their own lives." – *Professor Michael J Collins, Georgetown University Washington D.C.*

"*Hamlet and the Psychotherapist* combines Michael Scott's extensive knowledge of Elizabethan England with his passion for Shakespeare's plays. This unusual story of time travel provides a new take on the mind set of Hamlet, one of Shakespeare's most intriguing characters. This is an entertaining flight of fancy. *– Emma Lucia Hands, Director of Drama Studio London*

"A modern multi-racial psychoanalyst holds the mirror up to Hamlet, but unexpectedly, in his virtual return to the past, what he sees is his own reflection. Hamlet meets Back to the Future in multiple quests for identity. Psychiatrist Jacob Fortune travels back in time through the portal of his mobile consulting room, to straighten Hamlet out and to try to avert the prince's final denouement, but his quest leads him to discover the real, but mysterious William Shakespeare and some of his acquaintances.

"The life of the psychoanalyst gets entangled with a galaxy

of fictional Shakespearean characters, historical figures and transhistorical intrigues. In the mirror that Fortune holds up to Hamlet images merge, come into focus and recede under the watchful eye of nonchalant time-traveller "Spikey" the cat. Everything comes to rest in the talent of the artist, and the process is mediated through the virtual consulting room that shuttles the perplexed psychoanalyst and his colleagues at *4 Psychoanalysts 4 U* between past and present, all of whom are caught up in fictional analogues of their own personal relationships. A spirited and inventive investigation of the many ways in which art and life interact." – *John Drakakis, Emeritus Professor of English at University of Stirling*

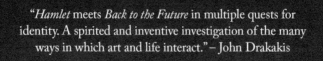

"*Hamlet* meets *Back to the Future* in multiple quests for identity. A spirited and inventive investigation of the many ways in which art and life interact." – John Drakakis

HAMLET
AND THE
PSYCHOTHERAPIST

A NOVEL

MICHAEL KERR SCOTT

EER FICTION
Edward Everett Root, Publishers, Brighton, 2022.

EER FICTION

Edward Everett Root, Publishers Co. Ltd.

Atlas Chambers, 33 West Street, Brighton, BN1 2RE, England

Full details of our stock-holding overseas agents in America, Australia, China, Europe, Japan, and North America, and how to order our books, are given on our website.

We stand with Ukraine. EER books are *not* for sale in Belarus or Russia.

www.eerpublishing.com

edwardeverettroot@yahoo.co.uk

Michael Kerr Scott, *Hamlet and the Psychotherapist. A Novel*

© Michael Kerr Scott 2022

First published in England by Edward Everett Root Publishers, 2022.

This edition © Edward Everett Root Publishers 2022.

ISBN 9781915115041 Hardback

ISBN 9781915115058 ebook

Cover design and book production by Andrew Chapman

www.preparetopublish.com

THE AUTHOR

Michael Scott is a noted theatre critic, and a widely published authority on Shakespeare and on Elizabethan drama. His books include *John Marston's Plays: Theme, Structure and Performance* (Macmillan 1978); *Renaissance Drama & A Modern Audience* (Palgrave Macmillan, 1982); *Shakespeare & The Modern Dramatist* (St. Martin's Press, 1989); *Shakespeare, A Complete introduction* (John Murray Press, 2017). He has previously published fiction as Michael Kerr Scott: *Arthur, Legends of the King* (Albert Bridge Books, 2017). He is currently Fellow and Senior Dean at Blackfriars Hall, Oxford, and Director of the Future of the Humanities Project with Georgetown University, Washington, DC.

THE TEXT AND PERFORMANCE SERIES (24 volumes).
(Macmillan)

THE CRITIC'S DEBATE SERIES (22 volumes). (Macmillan)

When a real artist is speaking the soliloquy 'to be or not to be', is he merely putting before us the thoughts of the author and executing the business indicated by his director? No, he puts into the lines much of his own conception of life.

Such an artist is not speaking in the person of an imaginary Hamlet. He speaks in this own right as one placed in the circumstances created by the play. The thoughts, feelings, conceptions, reasoning of the author are transformed into his own.

— CONSTANTIN STANISLAVSKY
AN ACTOR PREPARES

To Maggie

PART I

CHAPTER 1

T he noise was excruciating. I thought my ears would burst. The comforting regular thump, thump of travel faded. I felt an undulating pressure, accompanied by a screeching, high-pitched whine which steadily increasing in volume, grew worse and worse as push, pull; pull, push I awoke, on the stone-cold floor, in my Virtual World.

I wasn't sure where I was, although I could remember where I was meant to be and why. I was here to change or disrupt the first performance of Shakespeare's *Hamlet*.

I half-lifted myself up, rubbing my echoing ears and looked towards the window. There was something amiss. It wasn't quite as I imagined. It shouldn't have been a surprise as Amelia, my Team Leader, had told me what to expect. My consulting room, she had assured, would be with me and all would be the same except for the floor, the look of the windows and the door to the waiting room, which would now open onto the streets: the windows were on one side of the room, the door on the opposite side. I had exclaimed that my consulting room was on the first floor, but she assured me that when I arrived it would be on the ground: a single-storey building, fitted with solar panel walls and roof, which appeared to look as if it were thatched, although on this she wasn't entirely convinced.

Still partly slumped on the flag-stone floor, I looked towards the door which, rather than the familiar cheap modern chipboard, was now in stressed oak or something similar. I pulled myself up and crossed to the leaded double panelled window and looked out. There was a large building towering above the rooftops. It was thatched and had a flagpole but no flag was flying. I knew what it was but didn't dare believe. I opened one of the panels and was hit by an appalling stench. I stood back, and the window swung in the breeze knocking into a passer-by. He shouted expletives at me as he lost his footing and fell onto the grimy road.

There was no tarmac, no cars, no vans, no taxis, no impertinent cyclists, no red buses, just a few passers-by and this rather rotund man, heaving himself up, mumbling about 'bastard aliens'. His language reminded me of a London taxi driver shouting at a cyclist or vice versa. But where were those 'bloody bikes' that weave in and out of the city traffic? And the metropolitan towers, bastions of success, wealth, prosperity and loneliness - where were they? The houses and rooftops facing me were familiar only through books, plays and films. It was as if they were from the Elizabethan set for a Shakespearean comic movie or a production of *The Merry Wives of Windsor*. On the other side, a little lower down what I'd call a 'lane' rather than a 'street', was a bundle of rags. A woman was looking at it suspiciously, before giving it a wide berth. My attention turned back to the man who had been 'floored' by my window. He was now looking at me, having dusted himself down.

I apologised explaining that I didn't know what I was doing. It was a lame thing to say especially as he exclaimed that I had opened a 'damned window' onto a busy street. The street didn't look particularly busy to me, although it was dirty and certainly smelt of urine, shit and decay, with even the corrupting waft of death but without that antiseptic smell of the laboratory. I looked again at the bundle of rags – man or woman sized. Even the dogs were keeping clear. The rotund man interrupted my stare and candidly asked me if I were mad. I apologised and told him that I had only just arrived.

He had a red face and ginger hair and was probably in his mid-forties. He shrugged, saying there was no damage done and went to move on, but I stopped him by asking about the building with the flagpole, peering over the rooftops. He confirmed that it was the new Globe Theatre in Maiden Lane. I grimaced at a particular waft of stench at which he laughed telling me it was from the river on the far side of my house. He then rummaged in the leather bag at his side and produced a flier promoting the Lord Chamberlain's men in *Hamlet*, by William Shakespeare.

"You look like a sixpenny man. I can get you a sixpenny place for five if you want! Just let me know. I pass by most days. I thought something new must be comin' but not so fast. This was all waste yesterday. You must have put this house up overnight – fast work, well done but a strange building for here, or any place for that matter."

He stood back in the street and sniffed, looking up at the roof.

"That's funny, never seen anything like that! Is that how thatch grows where you come from? Looks like glass to me." He shook his head and tutting remarked, "Glass is expensive; not many windows round here with glass. Never seen a glass roof before; not in all my life. Plenty with grass but not with glass!" He laughed, "People must have money where you come from."

He peered at me while smiling suspiciously.

I had pinpointed a Norfolk-type drawl in his speech, but not wishing to explain the arrival of my consulting room nor myself, I focused on the subject of the proposed performance,

"Thank you, I'd love to go...... when is it on?"

He made to walk away but turned to say that the company was on tour but would be back before too long. He'd let me know. But, he added, that if they didn't move that poxy corpse up the road soon, there'd be no one to go to the theatre. He glanced back at the bundle of rags, commenting that the carters, were on their way. I looked. Two ragged figures were trundling a cart down the road to pick up the victim. God help me, but I knew, at least, that the stench had wafted towards me from the river rather than from the poor sod that had died in the street.

I turned back. The man was still gazing at me, examining me again as if I were an 'alien', in the modern sense of the word, rather than the Elizabethan one, where it referred to someone from another country.

I interrupted his stare with, "Do you work at the theatre?" I hoped that he might prove useful for me to know.

He laughed, saying that he partly owned it. My mind quickly went through the names of the six shareholders and settled on the one that seemed to be a manager of some sort, as well as an actor.

"You aren't Augustine Phillips, are you?"

Surprised, he confirmed that he was and returned to the window. I leaned out of the window to shake his hand, saying I was delighted to meet him. I then asked him to give Hamlet a message,

"Would you please tell him that Jacob has arrived."

He was now looking me straight in the face, laughing with some disbelief.

"Jacob? Ha! Have you brought your ladder with you?"

I panicked a little since my mode of transport had been frivolously labelled, "Jacob's ladder" by Dafydd Owen, the Practice Manager, shortly before I had left. How did Phillips know that? But, of course, he didn't know it. He just knew his Bible, as did Dafydd with his Welsh chapel background. Was Augustine perplexed or was he faintly threatening? I needed to be honest but remain vague. I continued the humour,

"Yes. I came by ladder and that's how I'll leave."

"With or without Hamlet?" Augustine asked bluntly.

"I don't know," I replied.

I wondered whether he was suspicious that I was from another theatrical company intent on stealing the play, its protagonist or one of the boy actors from the company, but leaning closer he whispered softly,

"Let me give you some advice, Jacob. People of your colour can find it difficult in the City. There are gangs of youngsters that just don't like you because you are different, and you must be wealthy if you have travelled over here and have so much glass. Understand? The Queen doesn't like your type much, but she tolerates you. She's getting old – not that we are allowed to say that – and when she goes, Heaven knows what'll happen. Take care, my friend. If there's any trouble you get out of town as fast as you can or just come to the theatre and ask for me. If you're a friend of Hamlet's, you are a friend of mine. Meantime, I'll give your message to Hamlet and get you into a safe area for any performance. Good luck to you, Jacob – I like the name. It gives you stature…. a step up!"

He gave a raucous yelp of a laugh, winked and went on his way towards the theatre. I smiled. Perhaps he hadn't been as wary as I had imagined but merely perplexed. There are always good people around and maybe I'd been fortunate to meet one immediately on my arrival. I felt fortune was with me by name and circumstance. In coming here neither Amelia nor I had thought about the danger of me being of mixed race. But I would remember what Augustine had said. It was to prove useful later in my adventure.

CHAPTER 2

My name is Jacob Fortune and I work in a Practice called *4 Psychotherapists 4 U.* Dr Amelia Angel is the Team Leader and majority shareholder.

My adventure had started with, what I admit now, to be an audacious letter.

Dear Mr Shakespeare

As a Psychotherapist, I am particularly intrigued by the character of Hamlet, the Prince of Denmark. Some would say that he suffered from the Elizabethan malady, or what we might call severe depression. This ultimately results in the untimely death of both Hamlet and other members of the Royal Household. I would suggest that through an exploration of his psyche, we could prevent such tragic consequences, leading to a more satisfactory outcome for all concerned and changing the conclusion of the play.

But are you actually the author of this play and all the others attributed to you? I have my doubts. However, I now have the means to come to your Elizabethan London, where I can both help the Prince to explore his psychological issues and also find out if you are the real deal – the writer of so many sophisticated plays and poems.

That is my challenge!

Yours sincerely
Jacob Fortune D.Psych.

To my amazement I received a reply.

Dear Dr Fortune
  I have no interest in your ridiculous hypothesis concerning me, but Prince Hamlet, who was recently with me, has persuaded me to reply, accepting your challenge.
  Let the game commence!
  Truly yours
  WS

It was clear that I was already winning the argument. Firstly, he hadn't signed his name. Secondly, he wrote as if both he and the Prince really existed. He had been 'persuaded' by the Prince! What nonsense! And who was this, 'Truly yours WS'? I worked that one out easily enough: W(e the) S(hareholders) of the Globe Theatre!! I was on to them.

I felt like writing to some like-minded people to tell them to stick to their guns, in denying that William Shakespeare was the dramatist of William Shakespeare's plays. In my view, Shakespeare was merely a fictional creation of a group of Elizabethan 'capitalists', wanting to boost company profits!

I had gone a little too far in my letter, saying that I had the means to go out and meet Shakespeare in his own century. The truth was that the 'means' had been developed from the research of my team leader Dr Amelia Angel.

She professed that a dramatic character is not just created in the conscious minds of the dramatist and actor but their subconscious minds. It is there that the character lives, breathes, talks, works, loves, copulates, reproduces, falls ill, gets murdered or dies by some other means. Characters such as Hamlet, she explained, are an amalgamation of two conscious intellects and two subconscious minds, that of the actor and that of the dramatist, which coalesce. In such circumstances, Hamlet could, as a living entity, be given psychotherapy in order to save himself. If wisely counselled he would work with his psychotherapist, rather than the dramatist or the actor, who think that they have total responsibility for his creation.

To put it simply, Hamlet could exist and live in the subconscious Virtual World, which when you enter it through psychotherapy, is as real as the world, which most of us know to be our everyday reality. This would be an exciting challenge.

Amelia's theory was all quite brilliant in that it allowed someone to enter a Virtual World and within that space, meet with characters who didn't exist, either because they were fiction or because they were dead. If this is hard to understand or accept, that is what genius is about and Amelia is a genius!

Amelia suggested that I could embark on the psychological journey, under her tutelage and become Hamlet's Psychotherapist. But, you may ask, why Dr Amelia Angel didn't take on this task rather than me? Well, why did Neil Armstrong and Buzz Aldrin land on the Moon but not Michael Collins? Good question but in Amelia's case the answer may not be what you think.

It goes further back in that she had already 'landed'. She had already experimented, with hardly any back up at all, by becoming the psychotherapist to Hamlet's uncle, King Claudius. He, in therapy, revealed to her that consciously he wanted to help Prince Hamlet by appointing a psychotherapist such as herself to treat the Prince, his nephew, over the unexpected death of his father, King Hamlet. Unconsciously, however, the King revealed that he had murdered Hamlet's father, lustfully married his sister-in-law, Queen Gertrude, (Hamlet's mother), and was now determined to exterminate her precocious, wimp of a troublesome son.

Amelia realised if she were to take on Hamlet as a client, Claudius would attempt to find out what the Prince was up to, or in other words, he would expect Amelia to spy on the young man. She, therefore, agreed that his melancholic nephew should receive psychotherapy, but not with her, as that would lead to a conflict of client confidentiality. She suggested that instead, an experienced partner in her clinical practice, Dr Jacob Fortune, (me), who is of mixed race, might be asked to take on the therapy role.

She knew that Claudius would like the proposal since subconsciously he was fascinated with the idea of mixed-race identities and sexual union, but more importantly he thought that information would still come his way about the Prince's intentions. He didn't realise how scrupulously professional Amelia Angel is, or for that matter I am, despite admittedly my occasional naivety.

My mission to 'rescue' the Prince, before the first performance of *Hamlet*, was, I thought, straightforward enough, although others might consider it to be subversive. But in my view, it is the play *Hamlet*, which is subversive by presenting a theatrical narrative resulting in a socially manipulative conclusion. The multiple deaths of the major characters, including Prince Hamlet, at the end of the play, allow the audience to go home from the theatre with all their social, religious and political prejudices intact. In this, it works on an outdated Aristotelian principle of catharsis, whereby the emotions of pity and fear are engendered through the narrative and finally purged through the mass slaughter of the story's major characters.

Almost everyone in the audience goes home happy, in the fact that although Hamlet, the poor sod, is no more, he died fulfilling his duty of avenging his father's death. In his long-winded way, he has not merely, through revenge, satisfied the discontented Ghost, but in his mind, he has completed the task of putting a disturbing universal order back to rights. He thinks that the death of the King, his father, has actually put time itself 'out of joint' and that he, Hamlet, had been 'born to set it right.'

How foolish it is to make such a statement! It implies that the death of a king, by whatever means, has some kind of influence over the order of the universe. For generation after generation, we have watched the play and been manipulated to suspended our disbelief, thereby giving credence to such ridiculous nonsense. It is this that is the play's mischief!

In dying, Hamlet, after raising a myriad of questions about the relationship of immorality to mortality, love and betrayal, authority and abuse, 'being' and 'not being,' tells us nothing, but goes to his death, allowing Fortinbras, a foreign Prince with parallel desires for revenge, to take over his country.

Therefore, I had decided to rescue Prince Hamlet either from suicide or from assassination or from some form of misguided ideological self-satisfaction. In doing so I would alter the history of the theatre and maybe of the world...... and that was precisely the point.

Hamlet's questions had gone on for far too long, generation after generation. Was he 'to be' or 'not to be'? Amelia, like me, had decided that if we could rescue the Prince from 'not being' then the world might be a better place from that moment onwards.

To do so might have an effect on the entire history of civilisation. Such is the current historical conscious and subconscious importance of the character to Western culture.

I'd better introduce you to Amelia Angel. You may recognise the name. She is the one who created AVTT or to give its full title: *Applied Virtual Time Telepathy* for which she won the Nobel Prize. AVTT was a major break-through since Dr Angel proved, contrary to what the late Professor Stephen Hawkins believed, that people could travel backwards through time. She did so by using psychology rather than physics. Indeed, she went back in time and told the Professor, but he dismissed her as a crank. Yet I can tell you, that Dr Amelia Angel is nothing short of brilliant, constantly refashioning herself in the past, in the future or the present whenever that might be. I think she is quite wonderful.

Amelia is a not just a Psychotherapist, who is licensed to deal with the conscious mind, but a Clinical Psychotherapist, who is licensed to deal with the conscious mind AND also to delve into the subconscious.

It was this Dr Amelia Angel who now trained me in AVTT and who enabled me to set off on my dangerous mission to save Prince Hamlet from suicide or from him being murdered at the behest of his uncle.

I was to be the Buzz Aldrin to her Neil Armstrong, but we would both work without a Michael Collins if we could. To a limited extent, Dafydd Owen our Practice Manager at Ground Control had that role and would have to know what was going on but not his girlfriend, Maddie Parker, who is a dressmaker. She had already made Amelia's Elizabethan clothes, thinking they were for a fancy-dress party. She would now have to make my doublet, hose and other garments, supposedly for a similar event.

As for the other two members of our practice, neither Dr Ever Truslove, my lover, nor my twin sister, Dr Jackie Fortune - both experienced Clinical Psychotherapists - would be informed. Amelia argued it would be clinically far too dangerous to involve two other psyches at the start of this experiment, which if they were not careful, could result in, what she termed, 'hypnotic overspill' leading to visual hallucinations.

I would miss having Ever and Jackie around. Amelia would act as my virtual supervisor, but I would miss seeing her in the real world. This certainly wasn't the case with Spikey, the Practice cat, who didn't like me and never missed the chance to show his displeasure by spitting at me disdainfully whenever he passed me by!

I was fully briefed and trained and ready to arrive in Elizabethan London determined to accomplish my two-fold mission - firstly to discover whether William Shakespeare actually existed and if he did, to find out whether he was the author of the plays attributed to him and secondly, to save Hamlet from the end, which his creator had predestined for him. I had been assured by Amelia, that Hamlet had agreed to meet with me.

As to what happened, I don't have to answer any queries or defend my conduct to the media, my professional council, parliament or anyone else. Although controversial, we believed that it was all above board and done with the appropriate consent forms being signed. As a Clinical Psychotherapist, I am both a therapist and a scientist. I believe in fact. What occurred is what happened. I witnessed it and was intimately involved with it. In that I experienced it, I have documented it for you, so you will understand and believe it to be true.

CHAPTER 3

After Augustine Phillips had left, I waited in my room for a few hours, maybe even longer. I'm unsure since time had shifted so much.

When I woke from an uncomfortable sleep in my chair, I realised that my time had now arrived. I washed and dressed and ate some provisions that Dafydd had left for me. He had also furnished me with two cell phones, one for business and one for personal use, labelled PB and PP respectively, together with a battery back-up pack.

It was only then that I remembered that I'd left the charger, which worked off the solar panels, with my phones' attendant wires and connections, in the waiting room on the table next to copies of '*What Car?*' and '*House and Gardens*'. Just to check, I immediately opened the oak door, which led out onto the street, stood back from the smell, which was even worse on that side of the house. I closed the door having ascertained that the waiting room had not travelled with me, so neither had my charger. As I was later to discover this was to prove a significant inconvenience in more ways than one. I had no option but to sort all that out at another time. For now, I had power enough in each of the phones.

I heard someone approach, who paused outside my door and then knocked. I brushed myself down and called 'Coming'.

I like music in my consulting room, so I had turned on one of my phones to iTunes, using a loop. I'd chosen an R.E.M. song, which I really liked, called *Everybody Hurts*. Its lyrics were a bit too close to the mark on this occasion, with its message telling us not to give up, which I took to mean that suicide was not an option.

Just in time, I realised that it was possibly too pointed and insensitive for the first meeting! So, I fumbled in the pocket of my doublet - that Maddie had expertly made for me - and turned it off as I went to open the door. As I'd hoped, it was Hamlet. The game had begun.

Hamlet, dressed in his customary colour of black, took a step backwards,

"Good God," he said, "You're black!" To which I replied,

"Well, you aren't so white yourself!" He roared with laughter.

As he stood there, I put him right by saying that I was both black and white which I felt I had to be in my profession, as I made no judgements about anyone whatever their race, gender, creed or social standing.

"Good man!" he responded shaking my hand, "My name is Hamlet. You can drop the formalities, no need for Prince or whatever, just plain, simple Hamlet. And you must be Dr Jacob Fortune a psycho something or other. My friend, Horatio, has told me all about you and warned me to take care, since shifty Uncle Claudius is paying for this psycho consultation, or whatever you call it, which he has instructed me to have! True?"

"Yes, well partly true except for……"

But he interrupted,

"Yes, yes I know but as I said to Horatio, 'If too many eggs fall from the nest, the cuckoo makes a mess of what he was doing'. Agreed? Yes of course you agree. You are a learnèd man and know all about cuckoos, don't you? Shall I come in or shall we stand here all day with people gawping at us, wondering what the hell I'm doing out here talking to a black man who managed to build a strange house on some scrubland in a single night? What do you say?"

"Yes, please come in." I replied as he strode past me into my consulting room and made himself comfortable in my soft brown chair.

He looked around the room from the seat he had taken.

I find that having challenging paintings in the consulting room distracts the client's conscious self from interfering with the subconscious, allowing the latter freedom of expression. Others disagree but for me it is important.

Whether it was important with this client is a matter for conjecture since I felt a little overwhelmed by his larger-than-life character. I suddenly wondered whether this Virtual World was one, which I could control.

He, however, was now up on his feet again examining a large, rather fine and richly coloured Picasso print. There was a beauty in the silence of his concentration as he looked at what for him must have been a very strange representation. He returned to his chair and merely said a little mockingly, "Peace also to you". I was impressed since the painting does depict 'Peace' being in Picasso's War and Peace series. What a perceptive mind the man had, seeing for the first time a work of Picasso! What a sensitive, learned Prince, he must be. This was going to be an interesting challenge.

As a Clinical Psychotherapist, I do not use Freud's couch technique but rather comfortable chairs facing each other. Furthermore, I try not to lead the client in a discussion. After opening pleasantries, I wait for the client to speak first. Sometimes this can take a while, even many sessions, but in Hamlet's case he started talking immediately asking,

"Jacob, if I may, I'm a little suspicious of your mission, so to speak, since I understand from Horatio, who has had a little talk with your Dr Angel, that you have come here to stop me committing suicide. Well, the thing is this – firstly I haven't yet decided that I will commit suicide. But in thinking about whether I should, or should not, I do actually utter a little phrase which I think will become rather famous. In fact, this little phrase, according to Dr Angel may become the most famous phrase ever spoken by anyone in the Western World. So, let's get our facts straight, right from the start. Whatever happens, whatever we decide, I will still say, 'To be or not to be that is the question'. So, there we are. I've said it so that has sorted out that problem without it becoming one.

Now, secondly, you need to know the reason why I am using this phrase. It is because you are absolutely right. I am contemplating taking my own life. Wouldn't you if you found out that your uncle had murdered the King, your father; making himself king by usurping the throne from the true heir, myself; married my mother, the Queen, whom he is fucking on a regular basis as the whole world knows? Furthermore, in my place, wouldn't you be a little more than weary when the said uncle has the effrontery to then declare me his own heir whilst almost simultaneously, accusing me, in front of the whole court, of adolescent melancholy and bad temper, both of which he implies, prove that I wasn't fit to be a King in the first place? He thereby tries subtly to justify his illegal and audacious act of usurpation, does he not? And damn it, in addition to all of that, he has prohibited my return to my vibrant, radical, Protestant University in Wittenberg, whilst allowing my girlfriend's brother, Laertes, to go back to his pathetic, conservative Papist University in Paris.

So, what that I'm his heir and bloody Laertes is only the First Minister's son, which means that his sister, my girlfriend Ophelia, can't be my wife because although she is good enough to love, she isn't royal enough for me to marry. This means we are destined to have a family of bastards whilst I'll be forced to marry someone with a name like Beatrice.

King Claudius has also made peace with the King of

Norway and he has granted Norway's nephew, Fortinbras, - whose pugnacious father was justly slain without mercy by my father King Hamlet, on the day of my birth - permission to cross our Danish lands to invade Poland! Is the man stark raving mad? I tell you this will end with Fortinbras taking the Danish throne if we aren't careful, leaving all of us lying slaughtered at his feet. And then Jacob, to cap it all, some pithy dramatist has made it all public by creating a play, which will apparently be seen by generation after generation. It is an outrage."

Hamlet breathed heavily, tapping his right foot on the ground whilst crossing his left leg over the right, rubbing it in an agitated manner. I, of course, recognized the posture as one of self-comforting, which wasn't surprising after such a tirade.

Clinical Psychotherapists are trained in spotting such visual signals!

I felt it was a good beginning, but we were still in the realms of the conscious rather than the subconscious mind. Nevertheless, his honesty had given me something to work on.

What was going on subconsciously here: sexual insecurity perhaps manifested by a distributed alpha male envy of King Claudius, Fortinbras and/or of his own father? And what about his mother?

As I confess that I'm not a Freudian, perhaps I shouldn't go into Mother-Son sexual relationships as it is usually a cul-de-sac. Yet Hamlet had raised the issue using the word 'fucking', which was a surprise in one so supposedly refined as the Prince of Denmark, but then I surmised that this wasn't considered an offensive word as it is now.

What he said about a supposed prohibition of marriage was also interesting. This, he stated, would lead to the illegitimacy of any children. That I realised could correspond to his situation as being denied the throne not only by the ascendancy of Claudius but also by Claudius' marriage to Hamlet's mother, Gertrude.

What if they produced an heir for Claudius? Had she gone through the menopause? Not necessarily, if she had only been fourteen when she had married King Hamlet.

Here we had a classic Freudian paradigm which inevitably linked Ophelia to Gertrude, both prohibited from being his wife in favour of Beatrice, for whom I felt great sorrow, whoever she happened to be. What did he have against that name? There are many that are far worse.

I didn't say anything but merely waited. He shifted a little uncomfortably on his chair and swept his face with his hand. He was agitated tending towards conscious verbal aggression. I needed to calm him down as he continued, leading us into a near-perfect stichomythia exchange, as follows:

"Did you know I'm contemplating suicide?"

"Yes, I knew you were contemplating suicide".

"Who told you?"

"You told me".

"When did I tell you?"

"When you asked me the question."

"When I asked you what question?"

"Did you know I was contemplating suicide?"

"Go, go, you question with a wicked tongue."

"Come, come, you answer with an idle tongue."

"You're a cheat, young man!"

"Yes, I'm a cheat, but aren't you?"

I laughed. He joined in, saying that he liked me and that I may be a cheat but an honest one. Any tension between us had been broken. He pondered for a while before asking me if I knew how he was going to kill himself. I resisted from saying 'with a bare bodkin' (a small knife). The stichomythia had been an indulgence to give him confidence, but I needed to avoid further references back into the play since that would privilege the conscious over the subconscious. We were currently travelling in the right direction and I needed to keep discipline.

The play wasn't the thing to trap the conscience of this would-be king!

Hamlet pondered for a while before questioning me some more, asking me if I knew how to boil an egg. When I revealed that I did, he asked me how long it takes. I said that it depended on the size of the egg, but usually, it would be three minutes after boiling started if you placed the egg in the water when it was cold, but five or six minutes, depending on size, if you waited for the water to boil before dropping it in, carefully.

"With a spoon or such like?"

"Yes." I agreed.

"I suppose it does depend, as you say, on the size of the egg, and how many eggs are being boiled at the same time?"

I was politic in my answer, "Yes, you may be right on all counts."

"I usually am," he laughed "it goes with the title!" He winked at me in a similar way as Augustine Phillips had and I wondered if the wink, which was more like a twitch, was some early Masonic sign or other. The question was whether I should wink back but as providence had it, my eye just seemed to twitch of its own accord and he nodded his approval.

These kinds of seemingly defensive off the track diversions are quite normal with my clients but may have some unknown force. Possibly his subconscious was harking back to the cuckoo in the nest. Maybe his inner sense of vulnerability was associating himself with an egg or unwanted infant, now grown to manhood, that Claudius was going to have boiled, i.e. exterminated, or maybe he was just hungry! It didn't matter. He was demonstrating an unexpected, wayward divergence in the conversation, which would help my therapy.

We had made a start and I decided we had done enough. So, I said that time was up. I suggested we meet again in two days. Although surprised, Hamlet agreed.

As he was leaving, he asked me how I was settling into this

new environment. I admitted that I hadn't been out of the room yet and that I could do with a good meal and somewhere to sleep. As quick as a flash he gave me money to get both, recommending a hostelry not far away owned by George Wilkins. He said it was safe enough, being next door to Wilkins' 'House of Pleasures', if I knew what he meant. I asked why it was safe and learned that Wilkins had his men on duty to look after the women and to eject the drunks. He then told me where it was best to empty my bucket or indeed to relieve myself away from the consulting room without gagging over the smell. The Prince clearly knew his way around the area and was concerned for my safety.

He gave me what he called 'the Queen's Colours'. It was a badge that signified that I was in London on government business under the authority of the Queen herself. No-one, he said would harm me, since to do so to the wearer of the Queen's Colours, could be seen as treason. Similarly, the cony-catchers, con men who worked in gangs usually of at least three, to rob visitors to the city, would keep clear of me. They could be whipped or have their noses split or ears removed or indeed all three, for trying to deceive an agent of, or to, the Queen. I was therefore always to wear them so that they could be clearly seen. It guaranteed my safety as long as the Queen were alive but if there were an interregnum it would be best to lie low or to get out of the city altogether.

We shook hands as he left going down towards the riverbank. I wasn't worried that he would drown himself as his conscious mind was far too angry and confused to do that yet, if at all. I hoped I hadn't miscalculated and couldn't help calling to him, to 'take care'. Without turning, he raised his hand in acknowledgement and continued on his way.

CHAPTER 4

That afternoon I did venture out to Wilkins' tavern where I was able to buy a good bowl of mutton stew which I ate with a tolerable piece of black bread. A number of men came to find out who I might be. No doubt one was a cony catcher but on the whole, I think they were honest. This cony catcher, who was 'the setter' had the purpose merely of befriending me as a stranger. Amelia, as well as the Prince, had warned me of such crooks. The setter would buy the stranger a drink and chat to him, finding out where he was from and the names of people he knew. This would leave the visitor prey to 'the verser' who, primed by the setter, would meet the visitor as he made his way back to his lodgings. The verser would greet him by name saying, 'Hi Jacob (or whoever). It's a long time since I saw you,' or such like and would claim acquaintance with his friends or relatives, the names of whom he had learned from the 'setter'. In that way, he would gain the visitor's confidence and so lead him to the 'barnacle', who would finally fleece him of his money by a confidence trick, a crooked game of cards or such like. That was the usual process of the 'con'.

If I hadn't been who I am and actually where I was from, as

well as having been warned, I might have been caught like a cony, a small rabbit-like creature, in the catch. On seeing the Queen's colours and my clear suspicion, however, the 'setter' made his conversation brief and soon left the tavern, probably to warn his confederates but certainly the worse off for the price of my drink.

It was then that Wilkins, a tall lank egregious man, in rather shabby clothes, made his acquaintance with me. Seeing that I was on the Queen's business, he asked me no questions except whether I had lodgings. As I had my 'workroom' as I named it to him but nowhere else to sleep, he offered me a room in the whorehouse, which I could hire for as long as I liked 'with or without a whore,' 'female or male,' he whispered. I told him that I had a partner at home and didn't need a temporary replacement, at which he laughed, but I appreciated the gesture and we agreed on a price for the room and sustenance, morning and evening.

In one sense it was something of a mistake, since the straw mattress proved to be flea ridden, which meant that for some of the first night I slept on the uninvitingly stained floor. But give Wilkins his due, the next day he had the place swept out, the floor thoroughly washed down with some noxious liquid and a new mat provided. He also placed a cross on my door signifying that his employees were not to disturb me unless I should change my mind, which many of his guests tended to do. He said that some of his best whores would be interested in a man like me but that he wouldn't have me distracted from the Queen's business, whatever it was. On the whole, he kept to his word and I, with one exception, to my resolution.

That first evening there was a great deal of talk in the tavern about the hanging of a couple of Papist traitors at Tyburn across the river. A number of the drinkers had been to watch the event, during the day. The details were gruesome since castration and evisceration had occurred, whilst the poor sods were still alive. One by one each of the already hanged victims had been taken out of the noose, before they had died, in order to be butchered in the most appalling way. The cries of each were so great, as they were being publicly disembowelled, that some people in the crowd had shouted out, begging the executioner to finish them off quickly, while others who were clearly enjoying the spectacle, had jeered and shouted for greater pain to be inflicted.

I suspected that some of the latter were in the tavern drinking with me. I felt sick at the detailed grisly accounts that they obviously enjoyed discussing. Many in the tavern were content that the Papists had got what they deserved. I wanted to add "for the love of their Christian God?" but thought that, as an officer of the Queen, it was best to remain silent.

No doubt in Roman Catholic countries the same barbarity was taking place on Protestant 'traitors', whoever the Papist monarch happened to be. The concept of Christ's commandment to love your neighbour, even if they are your enemy, seemed to have been lost in the hypocritical fervency of their varying religious interpretations.

Professionally, of course, I am aware of the sexual pleasure that male and female may obtain from violent acts, whether they perpetrate them or merely voyeuristically witness them. I recognised that gratuitous violence was something not confined in time, place or history to the Elizabethan world but present still within political systems that sacrifice individuals and decimate families, communities and countries. But now I'd better come out of my moralising phase!

The next day I made my way back to my consulting room, passing as I did so, a black cat which hissed at me as I walked by. It reminded me of Spikey, the Practice's cat at *4 Psychotherapists 4 U*, which is looked after by Maddie for us. I tried to befriend the cat, but it spat at me and made it clear that it wanted nothing to do with me. So, I gave up. A few days later, I gather, it spat at someone a little too much and was thrown into the river by one of Wilkins' customers. I don't know whether it survived, but sometimes I thought I saw it chasing vermin into rubbish lining the side of the street. It was sad if it had died since no doubt it had helped to get rid of some of the flea-invested, plague-carrying rats. I was to become very aware of life's grim cycle in this society. This was in the context, not of political realities, but of 'the old woman who swallowed a fly'. Life was something of a lottery whatever we did to try to control it.

When I reached my consulting room it was evident that someone had been inside. There was a faintly reminiscent, perfumed smell. I'm meticulous about my furniture and my pictures and could tell that they had been moved and my cupboards searched but nothing had been taken. I wondered if it had been Hamlet's men because they had left the place so tidy. It certainly hadn't been a gang of 'roaring boys' or 'girls' who would often go round threatening people in the street. Of course, it could have been Claudius's people looking for my notes, but there was no way of telling.

CHAPTER 5

For his next meeting, Hamlet arrived on time. He was agitated and appeared a little aggressive but polite. He sat down and rubbed his mouth with his hand and then pushed back his hair revealing a broad brow. His eyes were darting this way and that around my room. He sniffed,

"Has someone been in here, besides you?"

"I think someone may have been.'

"Where have you been?"

"I've been given a room in the whorehouse next to the tavern, you suggested"

"Wilkins' place? Did you say where your workroom was?"

"I think he already knew! He seems to know most things that are going on".

"It was probably him then. It smells like him. He uses that sweet unction to disguise his personal stink. Bloody old hypocrite! They use it at the theatre to withstand the stink of the crowd."

"Well, you recommended him!"

He smiled. There was no doubt that it was that smell. It was cheap brothel perfume.

I was already on the defensive. Hamlet had taken control

of the conversation from the moment he had walked in, but that was no bad thing. He asked me how I had enjoyed my whore but didn't seem to be surprised when I said that I had taken board and lodging only with no night visitors. He merely grunted and then went silent. Perhaps he thought that I'd brought one of the prostitutes back with me. Was he testing me out or was it that something else had happened? I waited until he might speak again but I admit I was a little discomforted by his possible assumptions. I felt in my pocket to ensure that my phone was off and that no ill-judged music would disturb us.

Eventually, he came out with the statement,

"I don't want to talk about me. Let's talk about you!"

This isn't an unusual occurrence with clients who say that they are paying me and that I should talk to them as freely as they talk to me. It is a defence mechanism to keep the subconscious anxiety from breaking through. I have to make a judgement about whether to bypass the request or go with it. Whichever, I try not to get locked into a process of conscious determinism but sometimes by acquiescing, confidence is built in the client that allows for deeper revelations to be aired.

"What do you want to know?" I asked.

"Why did you turn down Wilkins' offer of a woman?" I remained silent.

"Do you have one back home or are you a man's man?" Still, I remained silent. He was in charge of this interrogation, which in its questioning might expose issues of his own repressed sexual preferences. He continued to taunt,

"Were you being faithful? Don't you think that as a black man, the whores are curious about you and how you might look and perform?"

My silence had irritated him, so his goading had become offensive, but it was all under control. I was back in charge. I told him that I was here to do a job and I wasn't going to allow myself to be compromised. He rightly sneered that I was avoiding his questions and being hypocritically moralistic. I had no right to be sanctimonious.

I accepted his criticism and told him about my relationships with my twin sister Jackie, Ever Truslove and Amelia Angel, all of whom I was with in the same Clinical Practice. He was quickly onto my reply as if he were intending to 'psychoanalyse' me, but certainly not by following any ethical code of respect. He asked me outright which of the two did I fuck, Amelia or Ever or did everyone in our Psycho Practice, fuck each other. I was surprised by his aggression and hesitated to reply.

"I understand," he said, "something is going on with you lot, which is causing you a problem."

It had become like a game of tennis between us. I realised that my own control of the set might be slipping. I decided that to confide more in him about my sexual and emotional relationships, whether fictional or not, might actually open him up a little, without implanting ideas in his mind. It was a dangerous backhand as I began by saying "If you want to know…." But he interrupted saying he didn't want to know. He had enough troubles that way of his own and then he immediately mentioned his girlfriend, Ophelia.

I had won the set if not the match.

I learned that he had that very morning broken off his relationship with her. He suspected that she might be spying on him on behalf of her father Polonius, First Minister to the Crown. If this was so, there was no honour either in her nor in her sex. She was no better than his mother, Gertrude, who had so speedily married her brother-in-law, Claudius, after the death of her husband. The reason proffered for this was that the union would maintain the stability of the State at a time when there was a possible threat of invasion from Norway.

The proof that the strategy had worked was that a peace treaty had now been signed between Denmark and Norway. But all this was political hypocrisy. The only question was how his mother had been persuaded to sleep with such a man as

Claudius. To have his sweaty, stinking hands lasciviously fondling her sacred body. She was defiled, and she would pay for it. Hamlet said that he would punish her for that, even if the Ghost had prohibited him from doing so.

"The Ghost?" I questioned.

His demeanour instantly changed. He looked around the room as if a ghost might even be listening to our session. He then put his head in his hands rubbing his cheeks with his lower palms, until sighing he continued speaking quietly, as if not wanting to be overheard, in what appeared genuine anguish.

"There is a Ghost in the castle. Others have seen it. Horatio saw it once. So, it must be real. I've seen it. It must exist. But it only speaks to me. Horatio hasn't seen it again nor have any of the guards since I saw it and spoke to it. But to me, it is never far away."

He looked around the room and I felt a chill as if something strange had entered my space and taken hold of the man in front of me. Surely, he was hallucinating and I was sharing in that psychic phenomenon, because of my proximity to him. Yet there was an eeriness pervading. The window began to rattle and the door creaked. Hamlet stared directly at me and then through me.

"Can you see him now?" I asked.

"No," he replied, "but he is here. Can't you feel him, Jacob? He is listening. He is commanding me to act. To do as I've been told."

"And what have you been told to do?" I asked. Hamlet appeared to have gone into a self-induced trance.

"Hamlet! Hamlet!" I urged again. "What have you been told to do?"

"Kill Claudius," he responded, "and then I'll bury him six feet deep. The Ghost is my father, you understand? Claudius murdered him, my father, the King, and then married my mother, the Queen. I'm not to kill my mother. The Ghost said that I wasn't to hurt her, but I'm not so sure. She was certainly involved. I know she must have been part of the plot. Why else would she marry Claudius, unless it was for lust, or survival, or power? Women deceive us all. I know because the Ghost appears to me when I'm alone with Ophelia. Maybe Ophelia wasn't involved, but as a woman, why should she give birth to those capable of murdering others. She must remain pure, unstained, even by me. When I go to make love to her, my dead father appears, lying in the bed between us. His face is decayed, but I know it to be him. I see it is him. I imagine it is him. He prohibits our love, and will always do so, while my mother is copulating with his murderer next door. It is disgusting, filthy, horrid, obscene. It makes me sick. There is a stench surrounding me, that makes me gag."

He paused, bent over in the chair, holding his stomach in pain, rocking to and fro. I thought that he might even vomit. He straightened. There were tears in his eyes and sweat across his brow.

Hamlet's right arm was again around his body, his left elbow on the arm of the chair, whilst he leant his head into his left hand, which rubbed at his eye in torment.

Was this the merging of mother and girlfriend within the psyche as some would immediately conclude? Was the son wanting sex with his mother for whom Ophelia was merely a substitute? If so, was his proposed rejection of Ophelia, a purging of the maternal infidelity by a jealous son? Maybe his taunts concerning his mother's incest with Claudius were actually self-revealing of his own incestuous desires. Maybe this was the way a Freudian may have interpreted it.

But no, to my mind there was far more to it than this. The issue wasn't only about Hamlet's repressed sexuality and incestuous desire. Clearly, he had enjoyed Ophelia's courtesies on happier occasions. I had no doubt, he had previously possessed a sexual confidence. Certainly, as revealed in the last session, the mother fixation was playing a role but could something even more significant be being revealed by the subconscious self?

I didn't dismiss the view that the Prince may have a 'Freudian' mother fixation, but I challenged that interpretation, wondering if his subconscious might have been working to make him and me now living in the grey area of the mind, think that he did.

Something was being held back and until I could crack that mystery, I couldn't help him.

More work needed to be done. He was a great danger to himself. But he was a danger also to and from others especially from the machinations of the King, who could not tolerate having such a wayward person endangering the status of the Royal family. Parallels, in my own time, came to mind. Royal 'accidents' happen. Evil political coteries and lean emaciated hypocrites, the Cassius people of my own day, destroy careers, reputations and lives, even of the most exalted in society, under the guise of the will of the people.

Yet the most important discovery I had made was that this Prince Hamlet, who had come to see me, wasn't merely some character in a play. He was real in the world I now inhabited. This was no game. It was a matter of life and death. I had been selected, predestined perhaps, to save him or to let him die, in this Virtual World, which we both inhabited.

Maybe his relationship with Ophelia could prove the means by which he could find himself and in that discover some peace. I hoped that he would return to that in further sessions with me. I wondered if he might tell me more about his thoughts than are recorded in traditional narratives, none of which had quite prepared me for what came in the next session.

CHAPTER 6

A couple of days later, Hamlet arrived at my consulting room in a melancholic state, brooding at first in silence. I waited patiently, until shifting his position in his chair, and looking directly at me, he earnestly said,

"I don't think I am, who I am!"

I noticed that his face remained impassioned. I nodded but didn't say anything. He hesitated and then began by explaining that he had become unsure who his father was. He had always believed King Hamlet to have been his father. But what if his mother, Gertrude, had all the time been having an affair with his father's brother, Claudius. What if she were the perfect actress dissembling in the overt signs of her love – hanging onto her husband, 'as if increase of appetite had grown by what it fed on' – pretending that she loved her husband. But she didn't and never had. Maybe, she had only married King Hamlet to gain the title of Queen, but it was his brother, Claudius, that she had always loved.

Why did Claudius always stay at Elsinore? Why hadn't he gone anywhere on matters of State or was it just simply because he didn't want to do so? Why didn't he marry someone else – a Princess of Norway or Scotland or England? Was it because he had all the time been really in love with Gertrude? As for her, was her marriage all part of a lifetime sham because she was sleeping from the start, not only with her husband but with Uncle Claudius? Perhaps she was even pregnant by Claudius, already carrying the unborn Hamlet when she married his 'supposed' father, King Hamlet.

Hamlet immediately made a denial of what he had just said but then retracted the denial. He was in a confused state as he started back on his diatribe,

"Surely not! But obviously, she liked love-making, which isn't something you really want to say about your mother!" and then asked me rather aggressively,

"Would you like it if your mother had been copulating with your uncle for years so that you didn't know whether it was your father or your uncle, who was your actual father?"

I replied that I wasn't the one undertaking therapy. He shrugged and immediately changed tack by asking whether I was following his drift of thought. I nodded and waited for what was to come.

If what he said were true, he went on to mutter, might it not be possible that - irrespective of whether his mother was pregnant when she married, - Claudius could be his real father rather than the Ghost, who wished for revenge for being murdered? But surely, Hamlet puzzled, if there is an afterlife in which all the secrets of this life are revealed, the dead King Hamlet could now know that throughout his marriage, he was being cuckolded by his own brother and that he, Prince Hamlet, to whom the late King was appearing, was not actually his son, but the son of his brother Claudius. That knowledge might have been the real reason why the Ghost was entreating him to kill Claudius.

Hamlet looked me straight in the eye and asked aloud, whether this fact was this poor Ghost's hell or purgatory or whatever the Church decides the afterlife happens to be?

From there, the Prince started to question me on my own

religion. When I said I didn't have one, he quickly glanced suspiciously around the room and told me to keep my voice down as I could be racked, even executed, for making such a remark in Elizabethan England.

His mind then darted back to repeat that the Ghost had told him not to harm his mother. That was the proof of the goodness of this remarkable King, his supposed father, who after death still loved the woman even though she had betrayed him throughout his life. Why else would he have instructed that she should not be punished?

Unable to remain seated as his imagination flared, the Prince walked to the window, but his fury was mounting as his thoughts ran away with the terrifying implications of what had started to become apparent to him. This must have been what he had been holding back.

It was almost too gruesome for him to think about. Could Gertrude have been having an affair with Claudius, for thirty years or more and no one knew? Who helped conceal it? Was it the Chief Minister, Polonius, aided and abetted by his late wife? That old bastard would have been sly enough if the reward had been right. He'd always been close to Claudius and no doubt, part of the payment for his silence, may have been that his daughter, Ophelia, would eventually marry the issue of Claudius' fornication.

This could have been an evil pact from before either Ophelia or her Prince (that is himself) had even been conceived, providing of course, they were not born the same sex.

Of course, now that King Hamlet was dead, Polonius would continue with the charade – 'Oh his daughter', he would claim, 'Could never marry above her station, could never take the Crown Prince, heir apparent, as a husband' - whilst years before the opposite had been secretly agreed between him and Claudius - that Ophelia and the Prince would actually marry. The two old men had been waiting for the moment when the case could be made.

Hamlet stared at me from across the room almost daring me to contradict him. This certainly wasn't the story as I knew it and it seemed highly incredible, but it was coming from somewhere deep inside his confused mind. It was still, however, his conscious mind that was working through the issue.

Further, I couldn't help noticing that he kept placing his hand on his dagger's sheaf at his side. I wondered if this was the 'bodkin' which might soon be 'bared' and if so how would I protect him, but more particularly me, from immeasurable harm?

He walked over to a rather neatly designed "Made for You" mirror on my wall, looked at himself and after a few moments' contemplation, stated that he knew he didn't closely resemble his father or rather the man who for the last thirty years, he had thought to have been his father. He then, as I expected, turned on me,

"Is this what you do in your psycho-whatever business? You put filthy thoughts into people's heads! You make us doubt who we are and what we are, whilst you sit there smugly smiling at our revelations".

Thankfully, his hand kept clear of the dagger. He closed his eyes for a moment and then came to sit opposite me again.

He had calmed down almost as suddenly as he had raged. He then confessed in a confused way, that in the depths of his heart or head he had often wondered whether his father was not his father but his uncle, and his uncle not his uncle but his father. It was so horrible because then, he had murderous thoughts, not about his uncle but his father or maybe about both.

But no, just in case I was wondering, he hadn't murdered his father, nor had he instructed anyone else to murder him. He said that I wasn't to think that. He loved his father or the man he had known as his father. He had never liked Claudius, Uncle Claudius, Father Claudius…. Father of the Nation! He laughed nervously and then began to get agitated again as his imagination conjured up more questions and outrageous fantasies.

"I mean," he said, "how did she do it? You could hardly believe it, if it wasn't true. My mother, the Queen, must have been sleeping simultaneously with the King and Claudius, moving night after night from one bed to the other. The poor woman! How exhausting it must have been for her. Once one copulation had occurred in Room A and the male had fallen into a post-coital sleep, she would untwine herself from his arms and leaving him snoring, trot down the long corridor to the other male and a second copulation in Room B until he too fell asleep. Then she would return to the first to re-entangle herself in his drowsy arms, who then with all the physical toing and froing, stirred, desiring more after his rest – a third copulation and dawn was still far off and so it could go on, all through the night, up and down the corridor, Room A, Room B, in and out of bed, in and out of her, night after night – for thirty years! No wonder she always went for an afternoon sleep in her private rooms whilst the King took his nap in the garden. Unless, of course, that was when she was also in bed with Claudius and never slept at all. Whatever, she must have had enough of it, but she wasn't going to give up the crown.

Finally, she must have said,

'Look here, Claudius, I've had enough. I'm getting older. I can't keep at it, with the two of you. You are going to have to sort it out or I'll tell the King or I'll get old Polonius to do so!'."

Hamlet suddenly stopped his rant and looked at me without any emotion at all saying,

"That's it. That's what happened. She made the decision. She was sexually worn out by the two brothers. She wasn't to blame. No wonder the old Ghost doesn't want me to hurt her. If she dies because of what they did to her, his sins would be compounded. He'd never get to Heaven. She or Claudius must have discussed it all with Polonius, who had kept the corridors clear all those years. Polonius advised on what could be done.

Polonius knew those who could do it, but he'd exact payment – the original bargain: an arranged marriage between Ophelia and me."

He paused, in total horror, before saying,

"Unless of course his payment was to demand ……. No, no, I'm not even going there. It would make Ophelia my half-sister! How dare he, a commoner, even consider violating my mother. She might do some things but not that. He would have been eliminated by either King Hamlet or Claudius if he'd tried to exact that for his payment. Not that I would have put it past the filthy wretch, but he wouldn't have still been here if he had. No, I won't go down that path. I won't think that. If I did, I'd have to kill him. Ophelia loves him. He's her father."

He placed his face in his cupped hands as he concluded,

"If Ophelia's father were murdered, she would go mad, just as I have and then what? Would she kill herself?"

He hesitated with his hand back on his sheath,

"Would she use a knife or a rope or merely drown herself in the river that runs through the garden where my Father-Uncle died?"

The Prince took a deep breath and swayed back and forth for a while as if in oriental prayer. I said nothing. His mind was still working with that push, pull; pull, push of psychic tension and struggle.

Hamlet gave a scathing laugh breaking the silence by saying it was such an irony because he always wanted to marry Ophelia anyway! But Polonius was mistaken in his blackmail, whatever his demands, which surely would have been financial. The old Councillor had been past regular sex for many years. It was certainly financial or status-driven, even though Ophelia, at some point, had been conceived.

He pondered a little longer before saying he was satisfied. Ophelia was not his half-sister, but his father could have been either of the two Kings. Whatever, everything had changed since the murder.

At this point, I questioned him on whether he was imagining too much, overthinking it and that this wasn't helping him. He was perspiring with the heat of his internal mental struggle.

It was of course all quite bizarre and far from the narrative that has come down to us. But to Hamlet, it was an entanglement between the belief in a conscious reality and the personal subconscious probing of the imagination to create alternative facts or what some may call the new reality. What in modern terms might be news and fake news. Could any interpretation have absolute stability? Would he ever know what had happened? Was there any such thing as truth?

I decided that was a good time to finish for the day. He thought so too and left as calm as he could be in the circumstances. We made a further appointment.

The notes and record of my sessions at this stage of Hamlet's therapy, read as follows:

In my professional opinion, although, the Prince was well into his twenties, maybe nearly thirty, Hamlet was displaying a form of late adolescent psychosis about which he appeared to be aware. He even asked at one point whether I thought he was going mad. I answered that I didn't believe so but clearly, he had many difficult issues on his mind which could be causing a sickness. He thought that was probably so but questioned whether we were making progress. He thought that we were because so much was becoming clearer to him.

I don't consider him to be bipolar or autistic. Perhaps others, because of his obsessions, would disagree, but they only know him by his representation, not having had the advantage of counselling the man himself. Perhaps he is in an 'active phase of schizophrenia'.

Hallucinations, admittedly visual ones which are rare, plus delusions magnified by his exalted view that he was above being merely the heir, had already pointed in that direction. There was a relative absence of facial expression but that was coupled with massive mood changes and the veering off from the main line of thought with erratic word patterning. Yet he totally believed in the virtual world he was creating as if the fictions of his imagination could be a reality.

Some specialists, who would consider medical intervention necessary, would have probably prescribed Risperidone or Olanzapine, to be taken for the rest of his life. Even if I had wanted to do so, these were unknown drugs in Elizabethan London. But it wouldn't sit easily with my view that psychosis is triggered by social contexts that need to be understood and confronted with the aid of therapy, rather than the drugs which dull elements of the mind.

Despite what I said in my notes, I had to ask myself whether Hamlet was capable of killing Claudius, or anyone else including himself, in his present state of mind. My answer was, not unless by accident rather than intent, at a time of absolute rage or in the depth of total depression. For the moment, I saw neither extreme. Yet there was a vulnerability that he could be manipulated by exterior forces, for example by Claudius, or by the fantastical, such as the hallucinatory Ghost, or by the psychic tension being created in an unknown situation between the conflicting forces within his subconscious.

I had to admit to myself and resolve to report to my team leader, therefore, that a situation might arise whereby his social context would release impromptu irrational or possibly schizophrenic activity, which could have dangerous, unforeseeable consequences. I believed, that the sooner we found a solution to disrupt the ending of the traditional narrative, the better.

It was however by putting all this together in my mind, that I stumbled on a way that I could rescue Hamlet from the so-called, 'predestined' slaughter. The seed of a solution had at least been sown in my head. I needed to be sure, however, that the solution I was considering would actually work.

As for Ophelia, the Prince hadn't added more information, although I noted that he had not specifically associated her with his mother, except for a brief moment of fantasy.

CHAPTER 7

A man went to a psychotherapist and said that he had started to believe that he was a chicken.

The psychotherapist asked if the chicken ever said anything?

The man replied, "You need to see a shrink, not me. Chickens don't talk!"

There is a truth embedded in this little story in that we psychotherapists can sometimes do and say foolish things. I am aware that I do tend to bungle things. Even my phones sometimes work against me. As I saw Hamlet off following the latest therapy session, I knocked my pocket and found that I was listening to Pink, singing about the sweetness of revenge.

Thank goodness the Prince didn't hear the song. It might have put ideas into his head about me becoming complicit in his desires. I was remaining detached, of course, but I had allowed myself to be drawn into his field of interest about my own sexuality or at least that of my partners in the Practice. The fact is, that I thought I loved Ever Truslove and that Ever loved me, but I had disappeared and Ever didn't know where I had gone.

You may wonder why haven't I used the feminine pronoun

in referring to my lover? It is not that Ever and I are in a gay relationship and that I am refusing to "come out". No, that would be too specific. Ever is non-binary, gender non-specific, believing that gender is a social construct. I respect Ever's view, as much as I condemn the betrayal Ever must have felt by my sudden disappearance. Ever rejects the pronouns 'him' and 'her'. Ever just is.

In that fact, however, I wondered if there were a means to understand some of Hamlet's problems. He was genuinely "he" but a "he" who was searching for the certainty of a personal identity maybe beyond words themselves. That identity, so self-assured when his father was alive, was now as ephemeral as the Ghost itself. He had even recognised that the Ghost he was seeing may have been from within himself. Was this a purging of his grief through fantasies?

In that respect was 'Shakespeare', whatever that conspiracy might be (which I still needed to explore), wrong to give his character so many words? The Prince Hamlet I'd met, needed times of silence to contemplate his life as it was lived, rather than to find it only in the finality of his death.

Earlier, Hamlet, had tried to turn the tables on me. He had wanted to psychoanalyse me, to probe me about my own predilections and confidence in my assumptions about myself – the caring, understanding partner of a non-binary identity.

My sudden disappearance from Ever's life must have had an effect on Ever. We all need and search for identity in partnerships. Mine was with Ever. We would laugh together, make love together, punning dreadfully that I was 'For Ever'.

But in coming to this virtual place, I had left Ever without notice. I had broken a bond of trust and that had now started to play on my mind. I felt that Hamlet had perceived it and consciously or subconsciously he had challenged me and was touching on something that I was hiding from myself or at least trying to hide.

Even before I had started on this project, I had begun to

fear that Ever might have been having an affair with my sister Jackie, whom I loved more than anyone else in the world, except for Ever. Jackie was an alter ego – another self. With me out of the way, the two of them might gravitate towards each other. Perhaps Jackie's normally repressed feelings for Ever may have been released.

You might say to console me, that I shouldn't have worried as I had only been away a short while but forgive me as you may not understand. Time, in the Virtual World that Amelia and I had created to reach Hamlet, and Time in the Real World that I had left, were not necessarily synchronised.

Ever may have already been waiting months for my return. Ever and Jackie might have thought that I had died. My disappearance was a mystery as was that of my consulting room, of which the door to the waiting room had been locked by Amelia. The room's apparent departure from Wimbledon SW19 had left a perceptual void on the outside of the building. To some, it was as if it had never been there, except that is for Merton Borough Council's planning department, led by Mr Gerry Smart.

He had received a letter of complaint from a Mrs Prendergast, who lived on the other side of the street, pointing out the unsightly gap – 'the size of a room' – which had appeared on the first floor of the 'psychiatric clinic' (sic!) opposite her house. Furthermore, she revealed that before disappearing, the outside of the said room had been altered by having 'crude imitation thatch solar panels affixed to it, about which, she hadn't been consulted and presumed the Council was unaware.'

This was something Mr Smart decided needed investigation and a letter had been sent by the Planning Department requesting information from the Practice Manager, of *4 Psychotherapists 4 U.*

I had received a text to that effect from Dafydd on my PP phone because for some reason my PB had lost most of its charge. On examination, I discovered that when previously I had played Michael Stipe on a loop, I had done so on PB, not PP, and when I thought I had turned it off in my pocket, I had actually only turned down the volume. I was lucky that there was any juice left in it at all. I checked PP in fear that I had made the same mistake in playing Pink, although Red wasn't showing on that phone. Green, however, was fading and the phone was asking if I wanted emergency Yellow.

But now was not the time to worry about my Real World problems such as phones, planning applications or the construction of my solar panels. However, my room couldn't function in the Virtual World, without those on my outer walls as well as on its newly constructed roof. I had no idea how Amelia had got the men to do that and when I asked her, she replied laughing, 'prefabricated, fitted, whilst hovering.' Nor could I dwell on my jealous fear that Jackie had taken my place in Ever's bed or Ever in hers. Such thoughts were an abhorrence. I determined to put them all out of my mind.

What I needed was a different kind of distraction rooting me in my Virtual World. It came in the form of Mr Augustine Phillips who, appearing at my window, asked if I would like an unofficial tour of the new Globe Theatre. I was thrilled to accept. I wondered if I might even meet with Mr Shakespeare but intriguingly, I was told, as the Globe was currently closed for performances, the celebrated dramatist had left the city. Augustine assured me that I would be introduced to him at some point on his return. But I wondered whether Augustine was in fact part of the corporate conspiracy over the existence of the dramatist and I was merely being told a tale. I remained silent on the matter, so as not to give my suspicions away.

Augustine was very excited when he showed me around the new theatre, which he saw as being revolutionary in design and structure. It was against the Virtual Reality code to tell him that it reminded me of Sam Wanamaker's inspired replica, *Shakespeare's Globe,* around the corner in New Walk, just about

400 years in the future, although no doubt, in retrospect, he would have been pleased.

He told me that the Elizabethan Globe had opened in 1599, with a production of Shakespeare's version of *Henry the Fifth*, which was seen not only as a celebration of the famous King but of the current Earl of Essex. The Earl was at that very time still expected to return to London in great pomp and celebration, presumably having been victorious in his Irish campaign, just as King Henry had returned following his famous victories in France.

Apparently, Augustine, in that first production, had played the role of the Chorus, who referred to the parallel between the two mighty warriors. He proudly spoke the lines again, especially for me, from the stage where they had first been uttered:

——————————————- But now behold,
In the quick forge and working-house of thought,
How London doth pour out her citizens.
The mayor and all his brethren in best sort,
Like to the senators of th'antique Rome,
With the plebeians swarming at their heels,
Go forth and fetch their conqu'ring Caesar in:
As by a lower but by loving likelihood,
Were now the general of our gracious empress,
As in good time he may, from Ireland coming,
Bringing rebellion broachèd on his sword,
How many would the peaceful city quit,
To welcome him? Much more, and much more cause,
Did they this Harry.

Augustine spoke the lines wonderfully with volume, wisdom and passion. I applauded as did some of the actors that had gathered round to see what was going on. He smiled and then gave me his customary wink saying quietly,

"Whisper is, that it is all up with Essex. He returned home with a truce but that is considered to be defeat. Heaven knows what the Queen is saying about it, if anything, which would be worse".

He shrugged and then as if on cue from something said, one of the actors, pushed through the others, asking, "Is this him?" – I can't be quite sure if that was it – but Augustine's demeanour changed.

What happened next is still very confused but another of the actors, who had joined us on the stage, spun me around, whilst a third said, "You leave our Hamlet alone".

I started to protest but they had gathered closely around me. Someone shouted, "Did you bite your thumb, at us sir?" I replied that I hadn't insulted anyone but, I saw that the same actor had drawn a knife from his belt. I cried, "Augustine, this isn't right".

It is said that you don't feel the dagger wound at first, but the thug thrust it into me with such force that I staggered backwards in immediate pain. I put my hand to my side and saw it covered with blood. I was bent over breathing heavily. I looked up at the man – a complete stranger to me – who had inflicted the wound that might end my life. I thought of Ever at home with my sister, Jackie, and cried out "Why?" as I collapsed. The last sound I heard, before passing out, was someone saying, "He's good".

CHAPTER 8

I came to, whilst being carried aloft, head hanging. The world seemed upside down. The bright colours on the ceiling of the thrust stage were a blur. There was a commotion all around me, apparently, four actors had lifted me horizontally above their heads and were taking me in a stately fashion, backstage to the tiring room. I could hear music and what sounded like a cannon firing. I put my hand again to the wound. I felt the stickiness of the blood, but my head hit something and for a second time I lost consciousness.

I came to again in the tiring room and was given a mug of warm sac by a boy actor in the Company, who was named Nathan. He said that everyone was very sorry. The perpetrators were some new, visiting actors, who had come to rehearse with them. They thought that I had realised that they were just acting. I put my hand to the wound but found only a damp sticky patch on my clothing. Nathan laughed and told me that it had been a stage dagger which spurted blood as it retracted.

"And the cannon fire?"

"Stage business – as you had feigned death so well the actors decided to rehearse the final scene of *Hamlet*. You were being carried off stage to the sound of solemn music and of the cannon firing. They were very pleased with you. You didn't fuss at all, neither when they nearly dropped you, nor when they banged your head against one of the pillars. You acted ever so well as if you were dead."

I answered that I was dead as far as I knew.

After being told that the actors had all now gone off to the Bear Garden to watch the baiting, Nathan complimented me on what had happened. In his view, he said that the best acting comes when the actor loses himself in his part, becoming one with it. He had watched me. I was a natural. In the early days, they had had another black actor with them, who was just as good, playing a role in *Titus Andronicus*. Although I protested that I wasn't an actor, nor wanted to be one, he confided in me that Will wanted someone like me for a part he had in mind for a new play about a black nobleman who, having smothered his wife, commits suicide. I claimed that I wasn't interested, and in any case, I didn't know who Will was. If he was referring to Will Shakespeare, I didn't believe that he actually existed. Nathan looked at me sceptically, but remained silent, shrugging his shoulders and taking his leave. Rubbing my bruised abdomen, I left the theatre, walking in the opposite direction. Nathan, however, wanted the last word, shouting out to me,

"I'll tell Will and the others about you. Mark my words, they'll be interested."

I thought to myself, that this might be an opportunity to flush Will out – if he existed – so I shouted back,

"Tell him what you like but say that I'd like to meet him in person."

"Will do." Nathan impishly replied and ran off adding, "when he is back!"

I watched him go. Twice he stopped and turned back with a grin on his face. The second time, he waved and seemed to laugh before he turned the corner.

I took Nathan's mischievous laugh as an indication that he

knew something, which I didn't. He could be a key to me opening the door on the authorship question and once and for all, closing it off. His grin made me suspect this, or was it that now I was in Elizabethan London I was starting to have doubts about my conviction that 'Shakespeare' was merely a corporate construct. Maybe I was fighting with myself to retain my theory, which was somewhat different from those who question how the son of a leather worker, from a provincial market town, could have written such sophisticated philosophical plays. Their theories, in my view, stemmed from class prejudice. The proponents of these theories search for characters, like Edward de Vere, 17th Earl of Oxford, or William Stanley, 6th Earl of Derby, or the philosopher and statesman, Sir Francis Bacon, as the true author. This all seemed preposterous. They had been travelling along the wrong track, which, to my mind had been satisfactorily proved by scholarship. My theory, however, was different, and certainly contemporary. I was hoping to prove that the name 'William Shakespeare' was a business front or marketing construct. 'Shakespeare' was thereby a 'trademark' or 'logo' of a theatre, which in itself was of lower-class origins, having been built by an entrepreneurial carpenter, James Burbage, for audiences of all classes. He had done so for a company developed by him, his sons, Cuthbert and Richard, and some of their friends, who became shareholders of both the company and the theatre. One of these was Augustine Phillips, about whose priorities I was unsure.

If I had started to doubt, I needed more than ever to press on, to prove myself right or to accept defeat.

Nathan may have given me the key, but rightly or wrongly I believed that Augustine was the door through which, I'd discover the truth and vindicate my theory. I decided to wait until he passed my window on his daily walk to the theatre. I saw him the next day and so first letting him pass, I opened my window and shouted,

"Augustine, can I have a word?"

He turned, "You can have more than one." He laughed as he came back towards my window.

"Come in and have a cup of tea."

"Is that the lovely drink you gave to Hamlet?" He replied as he made his way towards my door.

On entering, he said that Hamlet had been talking all about my tea to everyone at the theatre, whilst they were all laughing about my supposed death at the hands of the visiting theatre troupe. He then started to laugh uncontrollably, increasing my embarrassment. He referred to the retractable knife and to my head banging against one of the stage pillars, which seemed to have been an incident of huge frivolity. I listened impatiently while I made the tea. Still chuckling, he watched me as I poured the hot water onto the teabag. He reckoned that if it was as good as Hamlet had said, we could all be sitting on a 'heap of money.' If I could get enough of those little bags to him, he could market it.

He drank the tea and immediately changed his mind, declaring that its taste would only be appropriate to aristocratic circles, princes and the like. At first, this proved to be an important statement, because he said that he had no entry into such society, and nor had anyone else in the company, not even Shakespeare, with all his airs and graces. I was later to find out that this was not necessarily the case.

However, at the time, my heart leapt because this seemed to prove me right. Shakespeare, if he existed at all, could not have been one of the aristocracy. The usual hogwash authorship theories were certainly out of the window. There were no aristocrats employed by Shakespeare's company, the Lord Chamberlain's Men, but he had mentioned Shakespeare, so I thought that I ought to tackle that issue immediately.

"What is William Shakespeare like?" I asked him. He told me literally - describing him exactly as we know him from the portraits that we have: high-brow, long side hair, penetrating eyes. He added that he was a good wit, affable and a bit of a genius.

This didn't get me anywhere, so I questioned him on the playwright's origins. He came out with it far too easily, telling me that Will was from a little town called Stratford in Warwickshire, that his father was a town councillor and in the leather trade, who had got himself into financial trouble. He said that some people suggested that Will, like his father, was a recusant catholic, but Augustine doubted it.

"Why?" I asked.

"Because the authorities would have investigated him by now and must have decided that he wasn't."

When I asked why he thought that, he replied that everyone was investigated. The Government had papers on us all. One of the signs that an investigation had apparently taken place, was the smell of sweet brothel-type perfume, left by the government agents after they had searched your house while you were out.

So it was, that I had gained more information from Augustine than I had expected. But as for Shakespeare's identity, I was no further forward. I asked if I could meet him. Augustine replied that he had already promised that it would happen on Will's return from Stratford.

He thanked me for the cup of tea. As he was leaving, he told me how disappointing it was that the Globe theatre was still closed, but they were hopeful that it would open soon. In the meantime, they were continuing to rehearse with the arrival of the visiting actors, who had given me such a fright.

"And do you know where they had just come from?" Augustine asked.

"No" I replied. "Why?"

"From Elsinore in Denmark. Would you believe it?" He replied with a laugh adding, "That's how Hamlet, the Prince of Denmark, knows them."

"Of course!" I replied in astonishment.

I was none the wiser about my own authorship theories, but nonetheless, I was happy that I had spent time with this rather jocular man.

CHAPTER 9

Hamlet arrived for his next appointment in an excited mood saying that a troupe of visiting actors had arrived. He knew some of them, including one, who was affectionately called 'the Player-King.' He looked at me quizzically, as if he knew something and I felt a little embarrassed about what had happened the day before at the theatre. I tried to cover up my discomfort and I told him that I already knew they had arrived and that I had met with them. He leaned back in his chair and laughed, asking me if my stab wound had healed and if my head still ached. I said that it was all a mistake and I hadn't realised what was going on. He generously reported that they all thought that I was a good actor, particularly when I hit my head against one of the pillars. I corrected him and said that it was they who hit my head against it.

"Well, no matter," he replied, "They are here and I am glad to see them."

His mood changed suddenly and he appeared to become lost in thought, even mouthing words to himself. I waited. I noticed that his face, that had been somewhat flushed when he arrived, had lost its colour. Eventually, he said that the actors had taught him a lesson. Apparently, the Player-King had recited some speeches for him, about the Greek warrior Pyrrhus, who avenged the death of his father Achilles, by killing King Priam of Troy. The actor was excellent in his diction and delivery. Hamlet reported that when it came time for the Player-King to speak of King Priam's Queen, Hecuba, in her misery, his eyes filled with tears. This caused Hamlet to ask me why this should be so. It was "all for nothing / For Hecuba! / What's Hecuba to him, or he to Hecuba! / that he should weep for her?"

Hamlet paused, and then continued saying,

"I cannot seem to do anything to relieve my grief over my father's death, nor can I avenge it, but I merely talk and talk endlessly about it, cursing like a peasant, but doing nothing to avenge what has happened."

"What do you want to do?" I asked.

"As I've told you, I want to kill the King."

"What's stopping you?"

"I need to know for sure, Jacob, that Claudius was the one who did kill my father/ my uncle - whichever he was. Now I know how I can find the proof."

I waited for him to tell me how. I didn't want to force him, but rather let him tell me of his own volition. His eyes were looking at the floor and then he raised them to look straight at mine, saying,

"I'm going to use these players ………."

"What? To kill him?" I interrupted. I was alarmed by his calculating coldness.

"No," He replied and then explained his plan, to pay the acting troupe to play a drama, which imitated the way that his 'supposed father' had been murdered by his brother Claudius.

If Claudius reacted to what he saw performed, Hamlet felt that he would then know for sure that Claudius was the murderer. Once he was sure he would be able to take his revenge.

I wanted to get deeper into his mind, so I asked,

"And tell me, why do you think that revenge is necessary and that you need to do it?"

His eyes were like ice as he continued to look directly at mine.

"Surely that's obvious." He said, "I cannot just 'seem' to be impassioned at my supposed father's death and outraged by my mother's marriage. I need to DO something. I need to shed blood, the blood of my supposed father's murderer, Claudius, now the King of Denmark. I need to mince his limbs as Pyrrhus minced the limbs of King Priam, in order to avenge his father's death. And as for my mother, may she see it all, as her new husband," he sneered loathingly, "is sent mangled on his way to hell."

Listening to this resolve, I felt sick. The Prince's melancholy was not merely one of wishing himself dead, or of being of no use to the world – or indeed himself – but one manic in its desire for violent revenge.

"Don't you see anything wrong in what you intend to do if the trick of the play works out the way you want it to?"

"Wrong?" He answered. "Do you think, Jacob, that I am some commoner? Vengeance defines nobility."

"Not so," I argued and suggested that invoking patience, forgiveness and mercy were the qualities of greatness. I asked him, moreover, if he had thought through the consequences of his actions. He continued to sneer at me, ridiculing the word 'consequences.' He said that he had no care for the 'consequences' and that he now merely wanted revenge. It was his duty to avenge because only by the shedding of blood, could there be the forgiveness of sin. He believed that the scene in the play, which he had written for the players, would confirm the King's guilt. Once that had been done, the next step would be inevitable – Claudius had to die and Hamlet had to be his executioner.

His face relaxed. He smiled and winked at me. Before I

could say anything else, he was out of his seat and through the door, heading towards the river as usual. I called to him to come back, but without turning, he raised his arm high acknowledging me. Helplessly, I pleaded with him to take care.

I realised that the situation was now dangerous and so I should have reported it to my Team Leader, warning her of Hamlet's psychotic change of demeanour. The introspection was giving way to possible action. He was gaining confidence in his determination to murder. I feared the worst but wondered whether Ophelia, because of her love for Hamlet, might be able to help me to stop him from killing himself. I decided not to send in a report until I could find a way to talk with the Prince's girlfriend. But how could I meet with her and where? I didn't know. What would I say? I should have asked Amelia. In short, despite what I considered to be urgent, I procrastinated.

CHAPTER 10

I don't know what Hamlet was thinking about our sessions, but I can remember my confusion. I wondered at times if I were going mad. I had after all, put my mind on the line entering this Virtual World, where there is the constant 'psychic tension', between the life instinct and the death instinct. In the next session, this concern for myself, as well as for Hamlet, came into even sharper focus.

We sat for some time, facing each other, without speaking, until he began by saying,

"I like being on my own. It helps me to think. I need to think." He paused before continuing,

"It is death that haunts me. It is not the means of death, but the quietness of it; the silence of it, which attracts me."

"Attracts you to 'not being'?" I asked.

"Yes, to the silence. But …." He looked up and sighed, "No doubt you are referring to my supposedly famous words of being or not being. Fine. That's good enough. I admit I like the idea of not being. I didn't exist before I was born, or at least I don't think I did, so why should I exist after I'm dead? If there was nothing before, why should there be anything after? And why, in between, should we have to suffer the anguish of what we call life? Why, Jacob, don't I just end it and leave it at that?"

I knew my answer would be risky but felt it necessary as we were making progress, so I took a gamble and asked,

"Why then, are you talking about it? Why haven't you just got on and ended it all?"

"Suicide you mean?" he questioned.

I reminded him that it was he who had started to talk about killing himself. All I was asking was why he was talking about it rather than doing it. This riled him and he snapped at me, saying that I knew the answer to my question, but nevertheless, to put it simply and honestly, despite what he had said, there was a doubt in his mind that all might not end with death. There might be an afterlife and an everlasting punishment from which there could be no escape. It certainly wasn't that he was frightened of the process of dying. He could kill himself easily with the bodkin at his side. It wasn't the pain. It wasn't the lack of desire or opportunity. It was rather the uncertainty, the nagging doubt, that all wouldn't be silent for him, once he was dead.

I questioned him further on this, asking him whether he did believe that there might be a god of vengeance and justice who would punish him. He looked at me in amazement and turned the question back onto me. Didn't I believe? Didn't I suspect that there could be something else, a different existence, one other than now, an almighty deity judging us all, once we were dead? I told him that I was being paid to help him and therefore I was going to avoid questions like that one being hurled back at me. He looked a little annoyed and shifted uneasily in his chair. Maybe I had gone too far and could lose him. I believed, however, that this was a critical moment in the therapy. If I pressed him in the right way, I might be able to get him to appreciate life over death.

According to some psychotherapeutic theories – I was seeing in him, the psychic tension between the desire for death and the desire for life. The death instinct referred to in Greek mythology, was known as 'Thanatos', as opposed to sleep, which the Greeks termed 'Hypnos'. Hamlet seemed to be conflating the two, when he referred to "that sleep of death". Hamlet's strategy, to have his father's death re-enacted by the players, was not just a means of flushing out Claudius' guilt, but of purging his own trauma. His struggle was in the attempt to reconcile Hypnos and Thanatos. From the former, he could awake and know exactly where he was, and reflect on his dreams, but from the latter, was there any awakening?

I reflected that this was all pertinent to my own situation in the Virtual World which I now inhabited. Would it be possible, once I was so deeply involved with my work here, to return to the reality of the Practice in the world that I once knew? Did *4 Psychotherapists 4 U* really exist or was it a fiction? When I left this Virtual World to go home, would there be a life there for me, or would I never arrive back, never find my way home? Maybe that home was no longer there, and never had been. Maybe it was an illusion and the push pull; pull push of my arrival, a dream, which was so convincing that I believed it to be true, just as much as I believed the existence of another world from which I'd arrived also to be true. So firmly was I entrenched, at this point, in my new life with Hamlet that it was the only life of which I could be certain.

I had to settle the doubts about my reason for being here. They were foolish. I knew why I had come: firstly, to prove my theory that William Shakespeare was a construct, a marketing ploy of some early theatrical capitalists and secondly, to persuade Hamlet neither to commit suicide nor go to an untimely slaughter. I needed to concentrate first on the Prince sitting before me wrapped in his angst and decide how I could help him.

Drawing on traditions within my psychological practice, could I rationalise an answer, in mythological terms? The antithesis to Thanatos (death) was Eros (life through love). If I could persuade the Prince of the benefits of love, then I would have a chance of him celebrating life which would frustrate the tragic ending. That is why I had thought of Ophelia.

The death instinct would only triumph if he remained focussed on revenge, with the result that more than one life would be lost. I had to divert Hamlet to talk about his love for Ophelia, but in that, would I be frustrated?

"What of Ophelia?" I asked.

Hamlet rubbed his eyes with the palm of his hand, his usual sign of distress and replied,

"What of her? What business is that of yours? I told you earlier that her father was working against us."

"Is there a chance that you are wrong in that assumption?"

"No." He answered emphatically and rose as if to leave the session. I couldn't let that happen for a second time.

"Hold it." I said, "Obviously something has happened. Let's take some time out, while I make some tea".

Hamlet walked across to the window and stared out in thought. I made the tea in silence and returned to the chairs. I asked him if he wanted to talk about it and after a while, he poured out his heart.

Ophelia had returned the small gifts, he had sent to her as tokens of his love, but he'd denied that he had ever sent them. It was at first petulance on his part, but she insisted that he had. She said he should take them back because they were no longer tokens of his love. At this he had grown more irritated and confronted her with his suspicion about her 'honesty'. He had ranted about the relationship between honesty and beauty and promiscuity. But in so doing he had been dishonest himself. He admitted that he'd said that he loved her but told her that she should not have believed him.

He had become more and more violent and abusive in his speech about himself and women who bred such sinners as himself. He was an appalling being, full of pride, ambition, vengeance and such horrid thoughts that you could not imagine them. He shouldn't be alive and nor should others.

He was suspicious of her father's hold over her. Beauty and Virtue were not one in her. She should join a convent or maybe a brothel, or if she went with a man, she should go with one who is a fool. Women, he had shouted at her, were inconstant and wanton, painting their faces, like harlots, to give them a false beauty. He wasn't having any of it: their jigging and ambling about. There should be no more marriages. All those already married, except one couple could remain as they were, but as for Ophelia, he demanded that she should get herself into a nunnery.

I listened as he appeared to repeat his tirade as a kind of confession of hatred not just of himself but of all humanity, male and female. He had apparently lost control of his rationality and yet simultaneously knew what he was doing. I had learned that the best way to deal with such outbursts was with a simple question, which I asked him,

"I understand but tell me, how did you feel when this episode with Ophelia was all over?"

"How do you think I felt? I was angry. She had betrayed me and I had betrayed myself."

He stood up and returned to the window. I waited for some time watching him, gradually calm himself down as if he were letting air gently out of a child's inflatable toy. His hand went to his eyes again. Restoring his gaze, he opened the window. It was a bright afternoon. I could see past him to the flagpole on the roof of the theatre, above the housetops. There was no flag, which meant that no plays were being performed. I imagined how it must have been normally on performance days when at around this hour the crowds would be in the streets, going to a play. My mind had strayed, but returned to the matter in hand.

"How do you feel now?" I asked.

"A fool!" he replied.

"Why?"

"I'm not mad but play at it and yet sometimes I think that I am!"

"And what of Ophelia?"

"I'll sit with her in court. And watch the visiting players perform the words I had given to them. When she sees the reaction of the King, then she will understand Claudius' treachery."

He thanked me for the tea and left me to ponder what I should do next.

CHAPTER 11

I t was at around this time that I felt the onset of acute loneliness stranded in the Virtual Reality of an age during which I had not been born. My client, likewise, was alone, devoid of friendship, with the exception of Horatio and myself. I noticed that he had not, for example, transferred his angst into deep hostility against me, as can sometimes be a problem for a Psychotherapist. Rather, I felt that there was a danger of a growing affinity between myself and this character, whom I was regularly meeting in my Virtual World. I suspected that I was even assimilating some of his characteristics within my own personality. He was suspicious of those around him at court, including Ophelia, just as I was, of those at home. I missed companionship. I felt lost without Ever and the suspicion, that an affair was going on between Ever and my sister Jackie, had started to become obsessive. I knew that I was constantly self-analysing. However kind George Wilkins and the people around me were, I still felt alienated. This was far from good. I had been pursuing my objective, of saving Hamlet from a premature death, but had become too involved in his story.

I thought, therefore, that it would be helpful to pursue my other objective and begin to uncover the 'corporate' identity of

William Shakespeare. A change of focus would give me some respite. Even though Claudius had not sent me any payment, I wasn't in need of money. Hamlet had made sure that I was well off in that respect. I decided to go down to the river and get a boatman to ferry me across to the city. He was a friendly character who told me that he enjoyed going to the Globe and was looking forward to it opening again. But when questioned he didn't know when that would be.

I asked him if he knew William Shakespeare. He said that he knew of him by reputation but had never met him. He understood that he lived upcountry somewhere with his family and added 'He's safer up there'. When I asked why, he told me that a number of writers and actors had been 'racked' or 'had their noses split' or even 'done away with in duels or in mysterious circumstances'.

"The theatre," he added, "was a dangerous place to be."

He dropped me off near Baynard's point. I walked up St Andrew's Hill past Blackfriars and Carters Lane to Ludgate and St Paul's Cathedral, which was a hive of activity in merchandise, sexual affairs and the active use of the pissing conduit running down its nave.

There was also a small theatre space, where the boy actors could perform plays. Although the Globe was closed, St Paul's was open for business. I saw an extraordinary 'tragedy' *Antonio's Revenge*. If I hadn't known better, I might have thought that it was satirizing Hamlet. It appeared to emphasize a liturgical need for ritual in the act of revenge, as if it were a Black Mass, as it was accompanied by chants and incense in the cloistered 'theatre' of the now Protestant cathedral. In this I wondered, however, if the dramatist was not only making fun of the old church liturgy but also the theatrical genre with which he was engaged. People around me told me that the playwright was a young but well-known satirist, John Marston, who had been forbidden to publish his poems anymore. His poetry had been publicly burned on the command of the Archbishop, for being profane. So, with "some help from William Shakespeare", he had started writing plays. My ears pricked up at this news and I tried to find the young man, but he wasn't around that day. I started to wonder whether he too actually existed or was part of the conspiracy.

That particular suspicion was laid to rest when a few days later, I went to Middle Temple and met one of the lawyers walking in the gardens, who turned out to be the young man's father. He said that he didn't know where his son was and didn't care as he'd brought shame and danger on the family with all his scribbling.

Later, I asked Augustine about the young playwright. He commented that he was 'a rather precocious talent' in whom some at the Globe had taken an interest because he was a writer who was attracting some of their wealthier customers away from their theatre.

This made me more suspicious as it seemed to contradict what I had been told at St Paul's, but Augustine made no mention of Shakespeare's involvement. Indeed, there was no news about the 'celebrated dramatist's' return. I was becoming even more intrigued about him, because I could find so little concrete information. I needed to determine the matter of 'Shakespeare's' existence one way or the other.

Just like in normal life, in Virtual Reality you wonder what the purpose of it all is. But something more had been highlighted, which troubled me.

It was as if Amelia, in sending me here, had in fact sent me to something beyond. She had taken our psychology to a new level. If, as some psychotherapists believed, individuals were in that constant psychic tension or struggle, between the attraction of life and that of death, Amelia had started to explore the pull of death itself. She had created a Virtual Life amongst the dead. I was alive, meeting and conversing with people who in reality, were already dead. Although they all appeared to be alive, I knew that they no longer lived. Was the loneliness I felt the actual experience of death itself, of questioning being or not being? That damned phrase again! I suspected that Amelia wasn't trying to save Hamlet, rather she was exploring life or 'being', striving against the irresistible reality of death or 'not being'.

But here in this Virtual World of consciousness within the subconscious which I had entered as 'a traveller', I was both 'being' and 'not being' because I hadn't yet been born and the people whom I met were dead but hadn't actually yet died. Here in Elizabethan London, it all made me feel extremely peculiar! Perhaps I was the one who was mad.

Death however was a constant reality. It was literally on the doorstep, in the streets and at places for public entertainment. The brutal execution of those two papist traitors, on the day of my arrival, wasn't an exceptional event. Public executions were commonplace. I witnessed some. They were part of the culture.

After seeing one of the executions, which took place outside the doors of a church, I returned to Wilkins' tavern and House of Pleasures, removed the cross from my door and paid George more money than I should have done. Later that night, as I had hoped, a young prostitute came to entertain me.

So, it was that I became potentially one with the Elizabethan dead, but nothing terrible happened to me. Wilkins had made sure that I wouldn't need to go to the Mercurial baths. The young woman concerned was certainly healthy and I paid her and George accordingly.

Did I feel guilt the next day about Ever? Did I wonder if I'd have a burning sensation in my loins and did I check my urine and my private parts for any abnormality, despite Wilkins' assurances? Of course, I did on all counts but there was no burning just the memory of excitement and pleasure.

Had I betrayed Ever? Perhaps I had done so as a matter of revenge. Perhaps Ever was with Jackie as revenge for my absence. Maybe we would ask forgiveness from each other;

possibly we wouldn't need to. Did Amelia think that all this might happen and if she did, would she care?

If Shakespeare did exist, I wondered if he had done the same and if he had asked forgiveness from his wife, Anne. I mentioned it to George, but he said that he never divulged his clients' names for which I should be thankful, as I wore the Queen's colours.

CHAPTER 12

"The experience of Time in the Virtual World is relative. The traveller through Virtual Time may think he or she, in the climactic fusion of the conscious with the subconscious, has instantaneously reached their destination. Real Time, however, has continued to move on at its usual planetary pace from the point of departure where days, weeks, months, even years may have subsequently passed in the virtual traveller's 'instant'. No one could be certain, not even from the monitors, how long the trip had actually taken until that first important cell communication from the traveller had been received. But more significantly, no-one understood the distortions of perception, which occurred when one looked back from the Virtual to the Real World and which one of them had become the dominant fiction."

    – **Amelia Angel,** *The History of Applied Virtual Time Telepathy,* (London, Angel and Kerr, 3rd edition)

Back home, Amelia had some answering to do to. Ever and Jackie felt that it simply wasn't good enough that Dafydd had apparently 'seen off' for now the officious Mr Gerry Smart, from the Council's Planning Department but that Mr Smart had turned up in the first place!

Dafydd had needed to say that the missing room was never there or at least not since *4 Psychotherapists 4 U* had acquired the premises. He had been forced to admit that the builder had included the room when he filed the original plans, copies of which Mr Smart possessed. But Dafydd argued, in his defence, that possibly the builders being builders had run short of money and never included the room when the premises were originally erected.

Mr Smart insisted that Mrs Prendergast, opposite, claimed the room had always been there and that she had seen men fitting solar panels to the walls and a roof.

"Well," said Dafydd with a knowing smile and shake of his head, "we are aware of Mrs Prendergast here, at the Psychiatric Clinic ('sic') and as you can see the room would have been on the first floor of a three-storey building, so how could she have seen solar panels being fitted to its roof? It doesn't make sense."

Dafydd paused before adding mischievously, "perhaps the room mysteriously just popped out, dropped gently to the ground floor, hovered whilst waiting to have a roof fitted and then flew away?"

Dafydd laughed. Mr Smart, puzzled, conceded that such an explanation was fanciful and went away to consider the matter some more. He would doubtless come back but hopefully not before I returned.

It was however my disappearance, which was causing the main problem at the Practice. Ever and Jackie were far from happy at Amelia's story that I was working for the Government on a secret mission. They should have asked whose Government, but instead assumed it was the UK's, not Denmark's, and therefore asked which branch. Unwisely Amelia said MI5 or MI6 as they were the first ones to come into her mind. Ever was infuriated by the answer and demanded to know the nature of the mission and whether I was in danger. Ever wasn't reassured that there was nothing to worry about. Jackie continued to question which of the two it was MI5 or MI6.

Amelia asked whether there was any real difference, at which point Ever became angrier and grabbing hold of an adaptor, that was sitting on the top of *House and Gardens* threw it at Amelia. Unfortunately, it hit Dafydd above the eyebrow which started to bleed profusely. Intense panic ensued as Jackie, going to help Dafydd, tripped over Spikey the cat, lost her footing and fell, banging her head hard against the door of my consulting room. I actually felt the cosmic vibration in my Virtual World. The cat yowled, Jackie was dazed; Dafydd was bleeding; Ever was still steaming and so Amelia decided to phone me, on my PB, in my Virtual World to prove to her colleagues that I was safe and sound.

I answered but Red was still showing. Fearing that I would lose the signal, I said that I'd phone back on PP, which I did. I noted Yellow, showing that I had very little battery time left, even on that phone.

Firstly, I asked if Jackie was conscious and was told that she was just a bit giddy. I advised paracetamol for her, plasters for Dafydd, and asked Amelia to hand the phone to Ever.

I told Ever that I was not with them because I was in a Virtual World, not the real one. Their world had actually become for me, a Virtual World, but no-one should worry as I would soon be back to make everything real again. Ever was missing me; I said I was missing Ever. We would be together again and then for Ever. The love pun as ever worked. Everything was sorted. I rang off. Ever apologised to Amelia, Amelia to Ever, Ever to Dafydd, Jackie to Spikey and everyone to Jackie. Dafydd, picking up the distressed cat, said that he would take it to Maddie for safekeeping. Jackie, still groggy, said she'd treat everyone to an Indian meal and a couple of bottles of Chablis.

The crisis was over, and I went to Wilkins' tavern where after a meal and a tankard of tolerably good ale I went to bed, having first remembered to replace the cross on my door. I dreamt that I had met John Marston the young playwright, who was talking to Shakespeare, but, of course, I hadn't, and he wasn't. Dreams are even more ephemeral than plays, or Virtual Reality: they are yours and yours alone.

CHAPTER 13

"Let me ask you a question," Hamlet said. I agreed.

"Where now are those two papist traitors, you keep mentioning, that were executed a few weeks ago?"

"Dead" I answered.

"I realise that but what do you think happened to them after they died?"

I asked why he needed to know, and he told me that there was a rumour doing the rounds that they were in Heaven.

I thought that interesting, if not a little dangerous, for those spreading the rumour but as I wore the Queen's Colours, I would certainly not be spreading the gossip any further.

I could only comment, as a Psychotherapist, by telling him that probably the most famous pioneer of my branch of science, stated that religious belief came from the same area of the brain as superstition. Many psychotherapists, in agreeing with him, didn't think that after death we went anywhere except into a grave or a fire or in the case of some, such as the body parts of those two unfortunate men, to different geographical locations. Meanwhile, their inner parts, some of which had been boiled, no doubt 'went to the dogs'. That was it. After death, many people from my own time, held that we no longer existed.

There were some colleagues, however, who believed that we had not come fully to terms scientifically with the concept of immortality or a supreme creator outside the Universe. So, religions of various forms still held sway and with them the concept of an afterlife.

In my view, the two papists, who happened to be priests, had gone into history. Whether they had gone into another life was something I could not comment on. It would even be dangerous to do so under the prevailing political regime, which had deemed them to be 'traitors'. That's why they had been executed. Of course, I added that the Pope wouldn't have seen them as such, as he would have regarded them as loyal servants to the church. No doubt that's why one day, he'll make them into 'saints'. For them, that would be an honour, about which they would be very pleased, if only they had known about it.

Hamlet shrugged and laughed. He thought for a while and then asked me outright why it was that so many Kings ended up murdered. I realised that we were heading back into therapy as Hamlet, giving me no time to answer, was as quick as a whippet in telling me his view. This, unsurprisingly, focussed on his father and his uncle. Further confirming my understanding of his mental condition, his mind was darting about from one issue to another. He was back obsessively talking about his mother's incest, Claudius's culpability, King Hamlet's life, a long period of deception and Polonius' involvement as both Plotter and Manipulator. He concluded this time, that although his mother shared culpability,

"the person ultimately responsible for my Father-Uncle's death by my Uncle-Father Claudius was actually Polonius, father of my girlfriend Ophelia! I wonder if my Father-Uncle in Purgatory has worked that one out, but you don't believe in Purgatory, do you? No, because you don't believe that I've seen my Father-Uncle since he died but I have. In fact, he is here now as real as you are. He is standing by the window."

I looked up at the window and had a momentary shock as I saw a figure there. He was a passer-by who had merely glanced in and then walked on along the street. There was no Ghost, except in the Prince's mind. Even if Hamlet had an extreme case of delusional paranoia, did that have to be the reason for him to die? I realised that before I could rescue Hamlet, I had needed to be convinced about his mental condition. That is why Amelia had set up the sessions with me. I needed to believe in what I was to do and to be convinced that he was mentally ill.

I decided to divert the Prince's mind onto something else by asking an old chestnut of a question in academic studies which is often satirized, dismissed and discredited, but would serve a purpose in this strange world which I had entered:

"Where were you Hamlet, at the time of your Father-Uncle's death?"

He answered that he was in Wittenberg, from where he wished he had never returned. He thought for a while before saying that if he hadn't returned, he wouldn't have seen Ophelia again and that even though she was Polonius' daughter, he still loved her.

He pondered but suddenly he got up from his chair and said that he had to go. The Court was expecting him, and he might be about to lose his innocence. The next time I'd meet with him, he could be a fugitive.

He shook my hand and gave me another bag of money. I was worried about what he had just said to me and I asked him what he meant. He said,

"I'm going to be late."

"Late for what?"

He didn't reply but raced off towards the river, which was in the opposite direction to the theatre.

I decided to follow him because I thought he might do

something stupid. Close to the river, in an area which often floods, he turned and walked quickly towards London Bridge, which he crossed, mingling with the crowds frequenting the busy shops as well as those that were just crossing the river on their normal round of business, no longer noticing the tar-coated heads of traitors, which were stuck on spikes along the bridge.

This is one of the busiest and most crowded places in London. Unsurprisingly, I lost sight of him and made my return to my consulting room. The wind wasn't in my face and so the smell wasn't too bad that day. The river was busy with boats going up and down and ferrymen taking the richer people, like myself across from South to North, or North to South. A few of them called to me, but I shook my head, returning to my thoughts.

A boy, whom I recognised from the theatre, was waiting at my window when I returned.

"Hey mister," he said.

I looked at him questioningly.

"The Prince says that you shouldn't follow him. He'll call on you when he is ready."

"Where is he?" I asked, but the boy ran away. I wondered if I were dreaming. Perhaps I was.

CHAPTER 14

To die, to sleep –
No more; and by a sleep to say we end
The heartache – and the thousand natural shocks
That flesh is heir to – 'tis a consummation
Devoutly to be wished. To die, to sleep –
To sleep perchance to dream.

Hamlet was in a sober mood when he next arrived. I was little better, as I was missing my colleagues and my home. I wanted to wake from this false reality, which appeared so real. I wanted, quite simply, to go home, but I had a job to do and I felt that, somehow, I was making progress. Would I be able to turn back the tide to prevent Hamlet from drowning in his own desire for revenge?

He was still seriously contemplating the existence of 'not being'. But what would that imply? Contemplation is not action. He was a Prince, a man of nobility, a man who considered himself as a 'thinker', educated at Wittenberg, the home of the great religious reformer Martin Luther. But what did all that mean in the face of the pain and confusion that was confronting him? Was he to fight? Was that the 'noble' thing to do? Or was he to end his torment and weariness through the ultimate act. The Ghost had instructed that he, Hamlet, should 'remember him.' As a Prince as well as a son, he had sworn to do so. He had even written it down. He said that I could read it if I wanted to, but I told him that there was no need. He was very agitated and pressed a further point, saying that he had also written of Claudius, that a man can 'smile and smile' and yet 'be a villain'. So it was with this usurper King, the murdering, rapacious, villain Claudius. He gave a grunting laugh and went silent for some time. I noticed that he was breathing heavily and was almost self-inducing a trance, as his mind focused narrowly on his situation. Gradually the breathing became more controlled and he became much calmer as he spoke again, saying that there was a way by which he could end all his troubles. He needed to decide whether he was to live or die. He laughed, remarking that it was a thought, which would make him famous, 'to be or not to be.'

"But let's set fictional fame aside. The fact is Jacob," he said earnestly, "I am a Prince and might prove my nobility as such, not in this anguish of wishing my uncle dead and my father revenged, but simply by killing myself with a stroke of a knife."

I stared at him without speaking. Although he was harking back on sentiments that he had exposed in earlier sessions, it was for him to talk, not for me to plant ideas that I had gained from my knowledge of a play, written 400 years before I was born. I needed him to keep talking and so I waited.

He continued eventually telling me that taking his own life would certainly release him from the world. Its effect could be like going to sleep,

"But there's a difference Jacob," he said, "in that when you sleep although you forget the world, your sleep remains a temporary measure. Death mimics sleep, except that there is no waking. We don't know what happens afterwards. The dreams in 'the sleep of death' might reveal a new reality, a new world in which we converse with others who are dead; those we have loved, like my father. That would be pleasant, wouldn't it?" He asked with a kind of vacant tone.

Again, I did not reply, since I realised that he was thinking through his words: talking to me but really only talking to himself. He went on to say that such a new reality, or new world, could prove to be far better than all the pain, trials and tribulations of the present one. And yet the problem was that we simply didn't know. No-one who had travelled to that world had ever returned. Death was an unknown, undiscovered place and the uncertainty about it made him, and indeed everyone, cowards. It was this that prevented any of us from doing the 'brave' thing or silencing ourselves forever.

He muttered these last thoughts as if I wasn't even in the room, but at last, he looked up and said directly to me,

"What do you say to that Mr Psychotherapist? What is the answer to my question, "To be or not to be?""

I was on the back foot. Of course, I knew the theatrical speech, which he had paraphrased to some extent, in the therapeutic surroundings, but he was here, in my consulting room, putting the question directly to me. What could I say? I had given up stability in my life at home, for the uncertainties of this experiment, to change something which often is considered to be set in stone. I had travelled to a different world, even one of the dead, although I knew I could return. I wanted to draw some parallels with my own experiences, but I had to remind myself again that I wasn't the client. I couldn't think of me and the enormity of my task. My duty was to him. It wasn't my angst that needed to be considered but his. I asked him a simple question.

"What did you feel, Hamlet, when you first started to formulate these thoughts?"

"Shame!" He responded in a flash.

"What do you mean by that?" I questioned.

"I was ashamed because after having these thoughts, I was cruel to Ophelia, as I have already told you. "

I pitied him because that episode was another memory now haunting him. He restated that he loved her and had now lost her forever. How could she love someone who had been so cruel and was permanently in this state of anguish? He hadn't wished to hurt her. He put his hands to his face and I think that maybe he was quietly crying.

"And so, do you think," I asked him, "That she blames you and that she hates you for it?"

"That's the point," he replied. "She doesn't."

"And does that make you feel more guilty?"

"I don't know," he said. "I was so cruel and she was so kind."

He then rose from his seat and walked towards the painting of Peace, which he seemed to study until turning towards me he said,

"I don't know anything anymore, except that I have a job to do and I intend to do it. I will prove the King to be a murderer and then I will kill him. That is my destiny, that is why I was born, to set the time aright."

With that, he sharply turned around and took his leave of me. I half rose from my chair as he left, and then sank back to reflect on all that had happened. As I wrote in my notes later, I still wasn't worried that he would commit suicide, not yet at least. The delusional fantasy of having to 'set the time aright' was, ironically, keeping him from self-harm. He had some kind of plan in his mind. I did, however, fear for Ophelia. It appeared to me from what he had told me, that she was deeply in love with him, and I felt that he loved her because of all that he had said. She wanted to help, but couldn't. He had gone far too deeply into himself, repressing the need to talk through his problems, with the one innocent person, ready to help him, through the antidote of love. That is why I feared for her.

As Psychotherapists, we sometimes suffer the phenomenon of our clients transferring the responsibilities of their actions on to us, almost as if it is we who have committed them. Indeed, psychology shows 'transference of guilt' to be quite common in society, diverting an acceptance of personal responsibility, by genuinely imagining that the offensive action was taken, not by oneself, but another. Similarly, instead of coping with our anger and disappointment, we transfer our emotions on to other people when we are distressed. We fail to act; we fail to give of ourselves and in doing so we egotistically promote our own sense of self-importance. This is what Hamlet was doing, focussing on his iconic fears and aspirations, by cutting out the most important element of all, the need to love and worse still, cruelly rejecting love offered to him by Ophelia. I was concerned about her. She had offered to help but had been dismissed by the Prince with his masculine notions of nobility, justice and revenge. I had failed to search for Ophelia whom I felt needed my help as a Psychotherapist. Like so many women, she was a victim of cruel and selfish male egotism, but Hamlet was my client. Although not the normal therapeutic practice, I once again determined to meet with her before it was too late.

CHAPTER 15

I f I made any mistake, it was this. Like Hamlet, I continued to procrastinate. I thought it would all work out but I should have tried to meet Ophelia immediately. I didn't.

A few days later I went for a walk, heading towards the theatre, which was still closed. I was now familiar with seeing and avoiding corpses in the road; silently waiting for the wagon. It was, however, the living victims which disturbed me. There was a man at a glassless window, gasping for water. I had a flask with me, which I took out and made to go towards him. But someone from behind grabbed my arm. It was Augustine. He told me that I needed to let the man die, rather than catch whatever disease he had. The dying man stared at my flask, mouthed something to me and then crumpled out of sight, below the window. Augustine let go of my arm, saying that he knew the man, who had once worked at the theatre.

"Is he dead now?" I asked pathetically.

"Maybe, maybe not," Augustine replied. "Does it make any difference? There was no cure for him. I don't believe it is your time to leave us yet. Go back home." Augustine left me and continued towards the theatre.

"Where was 'home'?" I wondered as I trudged back to the consulting room. There was a message waiting for me from Amelia, who seemed to be able to move between the Real and Virtual World with impunity.

Jacob.

I think that Hamlet is in trouble. According to Horatio, Hamlet went ahead with his plan and had the play performed in Elsinore, which imitated the death of his father. The King reacted and is furious. The actors fled and the King dismissed everyone so as to be alone. Apparently, Claudius paced the room and then tried to pray, professing his guilt to his god, but how could he repent when he was still enjoying the results of his evil? I know I shouldn't encroach on your professional practice, the Prince is your client and I mustn't compromise your relationship. But before the King's confession to his god, Hamlet was overheard, talking of drinking 'hot blood' in his desire for revenge. It was unpleasant, as he seemed to be allying himself with the occult, with the witches of old, who opened the graves of the newly dead and boiled their blood for liquor to drink. Hamlet, in my view, is dealing with matters deeply disturbing and hidden within his unconscious mind.

Jacob, you are in a dangerous situation. You are dealing such complex and intense emotions being displayed by your client, that as your Team Leader, I am concerned about your mental health, trying to cope with this on your own, with limited support from me. We maybe need to either involve another colleague to give you more supervision there or you need to abort the mission and return to the Real World as soon as possible.

Amelia Angel. Team Leader.

"Abort the mission!" I thought. "There is no way that I could do that!" I felt a sense of loyalty to my client. He was not a serial murderer. It was the corrupt nature of society that had spawned him, that made him have 'bloody revengeful thoughts.' This was a professional matter for psychotherapy. I still had a job to do and I would do it.

I ignored Amelia's warning, determining that through my professional practice I could prevent disasters. Of course, I did not blame her for giving advice, nor for breaking into my Virtual World, having exacerbated some of my own anxieties. It was as if a bad dream had disturbed my newly acquired existence. But what was the nature of this existence? Amelia had unsettled me and in doing so had raised a myriad of further questions. Intellectually had I forgotten, or missed something, during my training with her? How could you exist in two realities simultaneously? Members of a theatre audience could suspend their disbelief to enter the world of a play and yet still be aware of themselves, of the person next to them in the theatre, or of those they loved back home getting on with their daily routines. I realised that I was experiencing something like them, a multi conscious awareness of a variety of realities. In one sense, Amelia was right, I was on my own. Fiction was playing games with me, but so too was the reality of my normal life back home. Was Jackie in love with Ever? Did Dafydd love the dressmaker Maddie? How did I feel about Amelia, who always showed such a strong concern for me? I really needed to talk to her. Yet I was here in the Virtual World, providing psychotherapy to Hamlet.

I went out for a walk, retracing my steps on the occasion that I had followed the Prince. Why did he always take the road towards the river? Did he come here by boat – or think he did? Was he on a different plane of reality, that was intruding onto my own virtual existence? Did he exist in a variety of dimensions, from the performances in which he was to appear, based on the stories of someone who once lived in a similar reality to the one in which I had been born?

I took a circular route, doubling back as before, along the riverbank, where I bought some very expensive fresh water, from a seller on the baked flats of the Thames. We hadn't had rain since I'd arrived. It was mid-June, and inflated flesh was floating in the river. I wondered how many of these bodies would burst. I also wondered about death and what being dead must be like. My mind went blank.

I returned to my room at Wilkins' House of Pleasures and fell asleep.

CHAPTER 16

The next day, Hamlet burst through my consulting room door as if the Furies were in pursuit. He rushed over to the window, opened it, and looked frantically up and down the street. He closed the window and sat down. He was breathing heavily. I gave him fresh water, some of which he gulped down, before throwing the goblet across the room, spilling the contents everywhere. Patiently I picked up the goblet, refilled it and giving it to him asked what was wrong.

"I've killed Polonius!" He panted. "I didn't mean to but it happened." He looked at me with such sorrowful eyes, that my heart went out to him.

"How?" I asked. But ignoring my question he said,

"I've killed Ophelia's father. How can she ever look on me again?"

He had risen from his chair and started to pace up and down, going to the window, he looked outside again. I asked him what he was looking for and he replied that it was for Claudius' guards, who were pursuing him. It struck me, as I watched him, how fragile my Virtual World had become in relation to his world, which was that of the theatre. He lived within a play and although I could enter into it, to provide him with therapy, I couldn't ever be fully within his realm of reality. I was just an intruder. And yet, in a sense, I was here dishonestly to disrupt the narrative, within which he was confined.

It was just as Amelia had reported to me, Claudius had reacted strongly to the play, which Hamlet had asked the actors to perform and which depicted a similar death to that of King Hamlet. Claudius, at first, had totally lost his temper. Later Hamlet had found the King at prayer and had thought of killing him. But had decided against it.

"Why?" I asked.

"I wasn't born to send his soul to heaven, was I? I'm here to send him to hell."

I nodded. This all matched with what I had been told. He explained that he had been sent for by his mother and it was on his way to her chamber that he had seen the prayerful King and resisted the temptation to kill him. The Prince had entered his mother's room and she had chastised him saying that he had offended his father. She was referring to Claudius, and so the Prince had replied that it was she, who had offended his father, her husband, the late King Hamlet. They started to argue and he heard a noise behind the arras which hung in the chamber. He had immediately thought that it must be Claudius there, either spying on him or having just arrived to have incestuous sex yet again with Gertrude. Hamlet wasn't going to allow any of that. It was all too much for him. He realised that this was his chance to avenge his father's death. Emotion welled up within him. He thrust his sword through the fabric of the curtain, intending to kill the King. He felt the sword enter the man's body. He had done what he had been born to do. He had avenged the assassination of the Lord's anointed, King Hamlet. Claudius had fallen. The Ghost would be pacified. His own personal torment would be over. But then, he saw the body, wrapped in the arras, as the curtain fell down upon him. It was that not the body of Claudius, but of Polonius, his future father-in-law, a stupid interfering old man. Perhaps, the old councillor had got what he deserved. Whatever - he was dead.

The Prince fell silent and still. During his description, he had almost been acting the murder out again, to the extent of thrusting out his arm, as if holding his sword as he thought he was killing Claudius. He had gone into an ecstasy of excitement, an orgasmic avenging of his father's death. But now, in front of me, the Prince had fallen on his knees with his face in his hands, this time he was certainly crying,

"Jacob, what do I do now? I have failed. I have destroyed it all and now I am running away from the King's guards. If I am caught, Claudius will probably send me away, arranging a means for me to be eliminated."

I said, "If he does, and he tries to ship you away, be prepared for a confrontation with some pirates. Befriend them, because they will help you."

He looked at me quizzically and took another drink of water while I went to the window to see if the guards had arrived in the street. There was no-one there except a Friar, who was blessing a bundle of rags, the remains of another victim of disease or starvation in this strange world I had entered. I told Hamlet that there was no-one there, but a priest, praying for someone who had died. I then said that there was a way that I might be able to help him.

Although I have been considering it for some time, at this moment it was impulsive and quite outrageous. I had not discussed it with Amelia or anyone else. But I determined that now was the time to go ahead with it. If Hamlet was caught, Claudius would take control of the story, which I was trying to wrestle from its original design. For me, the Prince had to be saved and I could do it.

"Hamlet," I started to say, "There is a way, it is dangerous but......."

"I'm not interested." He snapped at me. "I'm on my own

and I'm running. I'll get away from them. You'll see. I'll escape and then I'll come back to avenge not only my father's death but also the consequences of the death of Ophelia's father. I'll beg her forgiveness. I'll be father and husband to her. I love her Jacob."

With that, he left the consulting room. I saw him from my window as he ran up the street, in the direction of the theatre. He bumped into the priest, who stumbled. The Prince stopped and helped the man up. That was the kindness of Hamlet, who, even in fear of his life, would help another.

"Hamlet," I called from the window. "I promise, there is a way to get you out of here."

The same priest, a Friar, now walking down the street, had got in the way of my vision, but he turned off not far from my room and I could see the Prince again.

"Hamlet," I called. "Come back. I can get you out of this world, which has you trapped."

"What?" he mouthed.

"Come back" I yelled, "and you'll see."

He paused for a moment and shouted,

"I'm coming."

With that, he started to run towards me. I moved from the window and prepared myself. As soon as he was to come through the door, without listening to a word he might say, or even looking at him, I would take his hand and together we would leave this Virtual World, returning to my own. Amelia had taught me how to do it and now was the time to go home. I stood by the door anxiously, closing my eyes and trying to find a space in my mind, which would allow me to travel. He arrived at the door. I said,

"Come in, give me your hand."

He did so. My return would be Hamlet's means of escape. I made my mind vacant, until I began to hear a noise familiar to me, from the time when I had come to this place. But now it was signalling my return to my own reality. I was hand in hand with the Prince of Denmark, whom I had saved. But I had forgotten that this was fiction and all was not as it seemed.

CHAPTER 17

T he noise in my head had become more and more uncomfortable until push, pull; pull, push, we arrived with a jolt at *4 Psychotherapists 4 U.* I felt such an exhilaration that it was hard to describe. Hamlet's hand was still firmly in mine. He had arrived with me as I hoped that he would. I had saved him, or at least I thought I had. It is hard to imagine the depth of my confusion as I slowly opened my eyes, and saw a blinking and bewildered Friar hand in hand with me.

"Who the hell are you?" I asked.

"My name is Friar Laurence, and I've come to ask for your help. Mr Phillips sent me. You see I ran away and I just can't forgive myself."

"Ran away?" I asked in utter astonishment. "Where did you run from?"

"From the tomb of the Capulets," he replied, speaking quickly and anxiously, "Romeo was dead and I pleaded with Juliet, who was just waking, that she should come with me from that awful place, where dead bodies on slabs lay rotting. Romeo lay on the cold floor close to her resting place."

I realised that this Friar had somehow got into the wrong story and indeed was from the wrong play. He was the priest who triggered the final tragedy of *Romeo and Juliet* by giving Juliet a potion, that would make her look as if she were dead, but after a certain time, would allow her to wake. It had been planned that her awakening would occur when her, newly married but banished, husband would be safe with her. Romeo would then, under the darkness of the night, take her away from Verona, a city from which he had been exiled on pain of death. But the timing went wrong, just as my return to my reality had gone wrong. Romeo hadn't been told in time about the potion, and in finding her, apparently dead, in the tomb of her ancestors, believed that she was actually dead, and in grief had killed himself. It was then that this meddling Friar arrived and once she had woken up, tried to persuade Juliet to leave the tomb. She, seeing her husband dead at her feet as it were, refused. Hearing the voices of officers coming to investigate what was going on in the Capulet's mausoleum, the Friar begged her again to leave. When she once again refused, he ran away, leaving her alone with her dead husband amongst her dead ancestors. It was then, that alone, she killed herself for the love of her Romeo. I thought to myself that it must have seemed an appropriate place for her to do so.

"But where is Hamlet?" I asked.

"Who?" The Friar asked in a confused tone.

"Hamlet. The man who bumped into you on the road near my consulting room. Where is he?"

The Friar went into deep thought, trying to remember the person with whom he had collided. We sat in silence, neither of us speaking, just as if inevitably we had started to settle into the opening of a therapeutic session, which I was hoping to avoid. This dismayed me. I had enough on my mind already, with one thing and another. He asked me if I was referring to Hamlet, the Prince of Denmark because if I was, he was most disappointed that he hadn't recognised the Prince. They were never usually at the theatre together.

"That's because," I answered, "You are in different plays."

He looked at me vacantly. I felt quite sick. How emotions can change so fast with the vagaries of life. One moment you are luxuriating in happiness beyond description. The next you are wallowing in confusion, grief and despair. I realised that by now, Hamlet would have been caught by the guards, and would be standing before Claudius and members of the court, having to explain how he had killed the Chief Minister, Polonius, whose body he had stuffed in a cupboard up a stairway.

It shouldn't have been that way. The young Prince must have been approaching the door of my consulting room, when the said room, containing the Friar and me, appeared to vanish in front of his eyes. What cruelty had I inflicted on him? I had gone into his world to help and now dejected, he would feel humiliated – despite his quips and bitter humour – and put under the guard of his so-call friends Rosencrantz and Guildenstern. He would then be made to go on a journey, which unknown to him, had already been planned by Claudius, to culminate in the Prince's grisly death on the block in a foreign land. After this, no doubt, his body would have been dissected by the court doctors of a foreign king, in the interests not of art but science. Surely Hamlet was not crafted for medical research but for poetry and the theatre.

I had wanted to disrupt the ending of this subversive play, but certainly not in this way. My job had been to save him. It would now look to him, as if I had deserted him by running away, just like this Friar had deserted Juliet, leaving her alone. I had failed utterly.

Good God, what was I to do now? What would I say to Amelia? I had lost Apollo 13. I had played the role of Jim Lovell and completely cocked it up. There'd be no Hollywood films made about me – the bloody fool who didn't check to see if he had the right passenger on board. And now what was I to do with this Friar who looked completely confused? He hadn't even recognised Hamlet…., the Prince of bleeding Denmark! He hadn't even heard me shouting out the Prince's name. He was so wrapped up in his own problems and yet……isn't that what I'm really about? Aren't other people's problems the reason for my profession and the purpose of my life? Instead of bemoaning what had occurred or wondering what the bloody hell Ever may be doing, shouldn't I be ready to help this totally confused cleric, standing bewildered in front of me? At least it was he, asking for help and not George Wilkins, asking me if I wanted to enjoy his latest employee, at an exorbitant price, before she was given the pox by another client. But why had Augustine, of all people, sent the Friar to come knocking on my door?

I said to him that he might feel a little confused but just to help us both a little, could he tell me exactly why Mr Phillips had sent him to see me. He replied that it was because of things that he had done, and not done, about which he was ashamed.

What, with the Friar's story, and with him sitting in front of me in his habit, it hadn't taken me long to work out that he must be a Catholic! It was all something of a giveaway, and now he was talking like someone who wanted to confess his sins. I explained that I wasn't a priest, but a Psychotherapist. Accidentally, for reasons I wouldn't go into at the present time, although he had arrived at my consulting room, he was no longer where he thought he was, but was elsewhere. Unphased by what I had said, he thanked me and enquired whether a Therapist monk was like a Trappist monk. I avoided the question; things were complicated enough already!

It was then also that my problems were further compounded because I heard voices outside my door. This, I noted, had turned back into its old, bland chipboard self. I looked towards the window, which I saw was back to being double glazed and facing rooftops. I asked the Friar to be quiet for a moment. I went towards the door and listened intently. It was clearly my bisexual lover Ever talking to my twin sister Jackie, in the adjacent waiting room. I moved even closer to the door. I could hear Ever saying that I might never come back and even if I did, their love for each other would last forever. Jackie replied that in not knowing whether I would return or not, enough time had gone by to presume that I was dead and that the two of them could live together for eternity. It then went rather quiet until the door creaked as one of them must have leaned back against it, whilst I suspect they kissed each other.

My world was turning upside down. The Friar signalled that he wanted something. I shushed him and pressed my ear to the door. I now clearly heard Amelia's voice. She must have just entered the waiting room and was introducing Ever and Jackie to a Mr Smart and Mrs Prenderghast. Their names seemed familiar but I had to think hard to place them. They were to do with the planning office, that was it. Mr Smart was the council's Chief Planning Officer and Mrs Prenderghast had complained that my consulting room had disappeared from the building. The voices had started to get a little strained.

"At last," I said to the Friar, "something good had happened since my consulting room has returned with us," which of course it clearly had, as we were sitting in it. He looked at me as if I were a madman but also replied that he was desperate to relieve himself and asked if he could go outside. It was the most opportune of moments. I told him to follow me. I opened the door and greeted everyone with a 'hello'. I took the Friar through the room and showed him the Gents toilet, telling him that he would find two different forms of receptacle inside, one for standing at and one for sitting on.

Having safely delivered the Friar to the toilet, I returned to the assembled group and said,

"Excuse me, but I'm in a private therapy session and your chatter out here has disturbed my client. I'd be grateful if you could relocate to the waiting room on the ground floor, where Dr Truslove and Dr Jackie Fortune have their consulting rooms."

With that, I opened the door to the corridor, and stunned

into silence, they all walked out and made for the stairs. Amelia whispered to me as she passed that I was wearing a doublet and hose. She stifled a laugh. The Friar came out of the toilet and I said loudly,

"Father, perhaps we could return to the consulting room, where we might continue to act out some more of your issues."

Amelia beamed at me and blew me a kiss, which she had never done before. Perhaps she, at least, was happy to see me back.

CHAPTER 18

W hen Amelia, Ever and Jackie returned, the Friar and I were looking out of the consulting room window. I was explaining what he could see in the street below. It was harder than I had anticipated. Everything looked so different to him, that he could hardly distinguish one moving item from another, the bus from the lorry, the taxi from the van, even the motorbike from the bicycle. In fact, what addressed his attention most, was a pushchair with a little child in it, being taken down the street by a mother. It was a strange phenomenon since it was as if he could cope with a small image, having a person on which to focus, who was pushing something resembling a cart, but as for the rest, it was all too great, fast and far from his experience or imagination to see it. We were distracted by the return of my colleagues, who had effectively seen off Mrs Prenderghast and Mr Smart. From the window, I saw the latter taking a photograph of our building before they shook hands with one another and went their separate ways.

Amelia had already asked Dafydd if he would look after my clerical visitor, whilst the three members of the Practice talked with me. Fortunately, Maddie had popped in, ostensibly to feed

Spikey the cat, but really to see Dafydd. She asked me about the fit of my Elizabethan clothes. I assured her that they were perfect for the project on which I was engaged, although clearly inappropriate for the current circumstances.

My colleagues, of course, were very pleasant to the Friar and hospitable, but there was tension in the air. Once Dafydd and Maddie had taken the Friar away, and Spikey was eating his lunch in my consulting room, Amelia, with some concern, asked why I had returned so unexpectedly and why with a Friar in tow. Jackie was trying to be jovial over the way I had arrived, which had put an end to the Prenderghast – Smart business, although she told us while looking out of the window, that Mr Smart was back again on his own, taking more photographs of the building, presumably with the room restored. Today clearly hadn't put an end to the matter. But what I found to be most off-putting, was Ever's apparent false enthusiasm in seeing me. I dislike hypocrisy and was seething inside so that when Ever clasped me close, I whispered that I had heard what had been said between Ever and Jackie about me.

"It wasn't serious!" Ever protested defensively.

"Yes, it was," I replied bluntly.

Amelia drew us all together, taking us, from the consulting room, into the waiting room to discuss the situation. I was asked to disclose what had happened and this naturally included a questioning of my decision, to attempt to bring Hamlet out of danger. I had bungled my plan, which meant that the Prince was now probably facing a serious predicament. In my defence, I weakly mentioned that I had said to him earlier, that if Claudius ordered him to be taken away on a boat, by Rosencranz and Guildenstern, he should be generous in befriending any pirates, who might attack them.

Rather than focussing our attention on the important matter at hand, this took us off on a time-consuming ethical discussion about whether, in Virtual Reality, I should have employed knowledge that I had acquired in my own reality, in order to advise the Prince about what might happen to him. This futile debate was a good example of the old question, 'What do you get when you bring 4 psychotherapists together to discuss a problem?' The answer, 'A problem 4 times greater than before!'

Finally, Amelia, seeing my irritation, took charge of the situation by saying that there were three immediate issues to sort out. Firstly, what was to be done with the Friar, secondly what was to be done to get the mission back on track concerning its two objectives, viz (1), to change the accepted narrative conclusion of the play 'Hamlet', preferably by preventing the Prince from committing suicide or by being assassinated and (2), to discover whether William Shakespeare actually existed as the writer of the plays usually attributed to him or if he was merely a corporate marketing construct, disguising the actual authorship of the works. Thirdly, she believed, as Team Leader, that it was important for me to have a colleague with me in situ, to act as supervisor, as is best professional practice. But as we were all aware, it would be inappropriate for my twin to supervise me, or vice versa, therefore the person who must go with me would have to be Ever.

There was an uncomfortable silence in the room, which Ever broke by telling everyone what I had overheard, but that it was a misunderstanding. Ever continued by saying, that I hadn't realised the personal hurt I had caused by going away without telling my colleagues where I was. Nor had Amelia understood Ever's feelings and desperation but Jackie had. Ever didn't wish to cause Jackie unhappiness, but as I required professional supervision, Ever was willing to go with me.

We all looked towards Jackie, the kindest most loving sister a man could have, in whom I had shown so little faith. She said quietly that she had always known Ever's love for me and that she had made herself a substitute in my absence, which she feared had become permanent as she hadn't heard from me for some time. She continued,

"Ever and Jacob are meant for each other and although it will break my heart to lose either of them and even worse both, Ever should do as proposed and return with Jacob if that is what is needed in the present circumstances."

It was a beautiful, generous moment immediately easing the tension. There were hugs all round. Amelia said,

"Then we are agreed. Jacob, you have to take the Friar back to where he belongs, which implies that you will also have the opportunity to rescue your mission. Ever then pointed out that there might be a further difficulty. I needed to identify at what point of time we should arrive back. If I arrived too soon or too late, in relation to when I had left, there could be a problem with duplication. I and the Friar might arrive when we were already there. We would get into such a mess as would happen in a Time fantasy story. But Amelia went on to stress, that this was not time travel as found in science fiction. It was rather applied virtual time telepathy, AVTT. It was a matter of the mind and therefore we needed to use our minds to move ourselves from one mental time zone to another. All the Friar and I had to do, was to keep to the formulas and discipline she had taught me. This would allow us to focus on a moment when we could arrive back together without anyone noticing that we had gone.

I thought back to what had happened and recalled that after bumping into Hamlet, the Friar had walked on, turned a corner, and gone out of sight. It seemed to me that if we could arrive back at that point, we might avoid difficulties. However, this would mean that Amelia would have to take the consulting room back, returning it to Elizabethan London, without anyone there knowing that it had ever disappeared. Ever asked if that meant that it had never happened. Of course, it had happened, we all agreed, because the Friar and I were the result of it, but we were putting things back in place, setting the 'time aright', so to speak.

There was a further question to be answered. How was Ever to join me as she had not been trained? The answer was simple. Ever would travel with Amelia in the consulting room, leaving Ever there as Amelia returned immediately to the Real World. I would then join Ever as soon as I had parted from the Friar. We all agreed that this was the best option, and so it was what we did.

The Friar and I arrived in the alleyway behind some houses next to my consulting room. I explained to the Friar that I knew his story but unfortunately, I was not taking on any further clients. I said to him, that he had done his best and that no-one would blame him as much as he blamed himself. There were other far weightier reasons, which had caused the deaths of both Romeo and Juliet. Therefore, he should try to forgive himself and lead the good life of a Friar in a priory. I did, however, recommend to him that he travel back home to Verona since Protestant Elizabethan England wasn't really a very safe place for Catholic priests. There was a tendency for them to be caught, hung and disembowelled. I also pointed out that he had just bumped into Hamlet, who undoubtedly would be happy to speak to him if he ran back quickly to engage him in conversation. When Friar Laurence questioned me about just having been in a strange place, with a group of people wearing unusual clothes, I told him that after his bump with Hamlet, he had lost consciousness for a while and must have been dreaming.

He took his leave of me and hurried off to see if he could meet up with Hamlet for a second time. They bumped into each other again as the Prince was turning the corner towards my consulting room. Hamlet did not come to my door that day, as the Friar, engaging him in conversation, delayed him. This resulted in the Prince being captured by Claudius' men, which was unknown to me at the time as I had made my way back to the consulting room. I didn't realise it would be a considerable time before I was to see him again.

In the consulting room I found that Amelia had already returned to join Jackie back at the Practice. Ever was waiting for me on her own, with some tea which had been freshly brewed and which we both thoroughly enjoyed. As we were sitting there, I felt something brush against my leg and heard a short familiar hiss.

"Is that Spikey?" I asked.

"I can't see him, but I thought I heard him too." Ever replied.

We looked around but couldn't find him. There were more pressing issues on my mind. I was less concerned about the cat than the Prince.

PART II

CHAPTER 19

Dear Dr Fortune

Some time ago you wrote me a letter in which you threatened to meddle with one of my best creations, Hamlet Prince of Denmark. Furthermore, you cast aspersions concerning my own identity.

Notwithstanding your interference and erroneous suspicions, which amused me, I replied accepting your challenge.

I understand, however, that you are now in Elizabethan London and have been counselling the Prince, endangering performances of the play, by altering its narrative. I am the person responsible for this play and I think that it would be courteous of you to discuss this with me. If you agree to my suggestion, I think I will be able to convince you of my identity by meeting with you, quill in hand!

I am in the country for the foreseeable future. Therefore, I will be unable to disabuse you of your misguided conclusions until my return to London. I will ask Augustine to let you know where and when we can meet.

Yours

W.S.

Augustine had come over to the consulting room, to give me this letter from W.S. I introduced him to Ever, who gave him a cup of tea. They chatted while I read the letter. I was irritated by the script. It proved nothing. W.S. could still have been '(W)e the (S)hareholders.' It had, after all, been delivered by one of their number who could well have been in on their conspiracy. The supposed author of the letter was again delaying any meeting with me.

On reading the latest letter for the first time, I said that I was perplexed by it and asked Augustine outright, who had given him the letter to give to me. He, of course, replied 'William.' But when I tested him on which William and when he had put it into his hands, he merely replied, 'Some time ago.'

We looked each other in the eye. He didn't flinch or blink and I took the matter no further on that day. Ever gave me some tea and took her seat. I pulled up my best chair. The tension between Augustine and myself was clear but Ever attempted to change the conversation by telling me about an invitation to go round to the theatre. I asked if the plague was still causing its closure, but Augustine surprised me by saying that the real reason that the theatre was closed, was not actually to do with the plague, which was always with them one way or another, but rather because of the competition from the boys' companies across the river. Their plays had so satirised the gentry, who bought the sixpenny seats at the Globe, that these customers had started to fall away. It had become fashionable for them to go now to the more exclusive private theatres in the city.

"But," I asked him, "Don't you and the other shareholders have a lease on the Blackfriars to combat all of that?"

Augustine, with a wink, said that I had obviously been talking with Wilkins and his friends and that I knew too much for my own good. He explained that there was a further problem, in that the company had a lease on the Blackfriars theatre and had been planning to make money from it and the Globe, but they had run into trouble with the neighbours and with the 'anti-theatre' Puritans. He was confident that they would sort it out, but that they had been forced to tour to make ends meet. Giving a resigned laugh, and again saying what a pleasure it was to meet Ever, he took his leave.

Ever was confused about our conversation. I said that I'd heard in the tavern that the Lord Chamberlain's Men were trying to create, what we would now term, an internal market. In summer they planned to run both the outdoor Globe and the indoor theatre at the Blackfriars, in competition with each other. Blackfriars could also be used in the winter, which would profitably extend their season. In this way they could curtail a little of the satirical competition they were experiencing from the boys' companies, performing in other private venues.

From what Augustine had said, the Lord Chamberlain's Men were still having problems with the people from the neighbouring properties, who were probably lodging complaints about noise, rowdiness, prostitutes, drunkenness and the like. Therefore, the Company was still being prohibited from performing at the Blackfriars, and with the financial problems at the Globe, it was putting them into debt.

"Oh, the neighbours," Ever said with a laugh. "It is like being back home with Mrs Prenderghast!" Ever paused, looked around and said, "It's exciting being here at last." However, what Ever didn't realise was that the lodgings where we would be spending the night was a brothel!

CHAPTER 20

I had plenty to think about that week. Ever's arrival was companionable but however broad-minded Ever was, Ever certainly did not like the sleeping accommodation that we had at Wilkins' House of Pleasures. I had heard of other places I could rent, not far away, in Paris Gardens Lane, and at the 'Elephant' in Horseshoe Alley. I promised to look into it. I also needed to follow up on the letter from W.S. but I had no means to ascertain if it was genuine as no address had been given. Certainly, there were people I had met who had heard of William Shakespeare and some even said that they knew him. I had no doubt a man with such a name existed but was he really the author of the plays? The letter was enigmatic. Ever pointed out that W.S. in saying that he was in the country, hadn't identified which part of the country. I expected it to be Stratford, but I would ask Augustine. The issue wasn't where but whether I should go into the country and try to find Will, rather than wait for goodness knows how long, for him to return to London. If it were Stratford, it would be a four-day horse ride for us, but neither Ever nor I were experienced riders.

The latest communication, brought to me by Augustine,

was a deliberate attempt to put me off the scent of the shareholders' capitalist exercise. Yet Augustine had been very open in telling me about the Globe's financial problems, which was the reason it was currently closed. I had assumed that it was because of the plague, but maybe the people I had seen dying in such terrible circumstances, was nothing compared to the major plagues that the Elizabethans had suffered in previous years.

All in all, my mind was unsettled and so I decided to do some more research into these matters. During their discussion over tea, Ever had agreed to help Augustine to train some boy actors in *As You Like It*. He had recognised that Ever was bisexual and experienced in one sex taking on the mannerisms of another. This experience was perfect to help the boys understand some of the roles in the Comedies they were to present. I wished to attend those rehearsals, but also to meet people from outside the theatre, in the areas close by, to find alternative accommodation.

That afternoon, we went to have some food in Wilkins' Tavern. I was now well-known and already seen to be something of an eccentric. I introduced Ever as my wife, who had come from abroad. This was so that the androgynous twenty-first century clothes didn't cause as big a stir as I might have imagined. Ever was far from pleased with my words, but understood. Wilkins, however, did take me aside to warn me that in the future Ever may be well advised to dress a little 'more seemly' for London. I resolved to find a means of obtaining the 'Queen's Colours' for Ever. But for the moment, as far as anyone else was concerned, Ever, as my wife, was protected. Even that, however, didn't stop them from considering Ever to be exotic, not least because of being the white 'wife' of a half-caste man.

We could easily get into some danger, which made us wonder whether we should await the arrival of the new clothes that Maddie was making for Ever at home, or if needs be, ask Augustine if we could buy an outfit for Ever from the theatre.

Nevertheless, we did pick up some information over dinner, about possible accommodation that might be coming available in St Helen's Parish, north of the river. At first, this was a passing interest until I heard one of the customers say that Will Shakespeare had once lived across that way because of his connections with the leather trade. That struck a chord with me because, in tales about Shakespeare's home, it had often been pointed out, that his father was in the leather trade, making gloves and suchlike. This passing remark was perhaps a first indication of how I could get to know the man, who purported to be the dramatist.

"Do you know Will Shakespeare?" I asked the customer, adding quickly, "And do you know what he does?"

"Of course, I do." The man answered, "He is an actor at the Globe: a quiet fellow but a good actor, although not as good as Burbage, who is a real actor. You know, an actor's actor and a people's actor. We all love Burbage."

"I understand that and have heard great things about him. I wonder if Shakespeare might be a dramatist."

"What's one of those?" the man asked.

"The one who actually writes the plays."

"Oh yes, he is a bit of a scribbler and his fingers are always black with ink and his name is often on the bills, saying that he is the one that has written the play, but who's to tell? They are all scribblers, dancers, singers, poets. They do the lot!"

My final question to him was whether he knew where Shakespeare might be found. He told me that the fellow often went back home to Warwickshire and then would be away for some time. I pressed him on whether this was a man that he actually knew.

"Of course, I do," he said. "He sometimes drinks in here and I went to court to take out sureties of the peace against him." I was aghast at this throwaway statement.

"And did you win?" I asked.

"Of course, I did. Haven't you ever heard of me?" he questioned, with disappointment.

When I admitted that, unfortunately, I hadn't, he told me that his name was William Wayte. I made a note of it and decided to contact Amelia to try and find out who this man might be and why he had gone to court to have Shakespeare 'bound over to keep the peace.' What had this Shakespeare done to deserve such an action? And was this the Shakespeare for whom I was searching? Maybe subconsciously this had also given me an excuse to contact Amelia again!

CHAPTER 21

No sooner had I sent my note to Amelia, concerning William Wayte, than a boy from the theatre knocked at the door. He asked if I were Dr Fortune and then he gave me a letter from Horatio, Hamlet's friend, for which I thanked him with a coin. The script actually was from Hamlet, which Horatio had forwarded.

Jacob

I have been very troubled since my arrest. Rosencrantz and Guildenstern have me in their keeping and we are heading for a port. I fear that they are in Claudius' pay, not merely to get me out of the country, but out of this world altogether.

We are just resting at present. Our travel has been barred by the movement of Prince Fortinbras' troops, across our Danish land, in order for him to attack the Polacks. It makes me think of my duty to do the deed I've sworn to do. As human beings we have to use the capabilities given to us by God. We mustn't let them rot, so why is it that I haven't yet avenged my father's death? I have been turning it all over in my mind, day by day, finding excuses not to kill the King. I see so many people, taking action over lesser matters than this one, which haunts me.

The army, led by Prince Fortinbras, is more determined than I am.

Each man could be going to his death, without really knowing the reason why he is fighting. The Prince appears to be a worthy man and bold leader, inspiring his men. He has found a 'quarrel of honour' to persuade them to follow him, whatever the result. So, they will fight for an insignificant plot of land, almost too small even for their battles and with not enough room to bury their dead. Yet I, who have every reason to take my revenge against King Hamlet's murderer and against my mother's incest, have done nothing.

Well, that is going to change. I am more determined than ever, that I will avenge the death of King Hamlet. I suspect that my so-called friends are leading me to a summary execution in a foreign land. They have secret letters for the King of that place. As soon as the opportunity arises, I will exchange those letters with ones I will write myself and authorise them with my Danish seal. Rosencrantz and Guildenstern will be dead by the evening of our arrival. After thanking the Monarch of that land, and doing some kind of trade deal with him, I'll return to Elsinore where I will relish killing Claudius.

I just want you to know that my mind is fixed. I trust you. I will do as I've said. I will send this note by one of my trusted riders, with other letters for Horatio, asking him to deliver it to you.

Hamlet.

I pondered about the letter and showed it to Ever. There wasn't anything new in it. There was no telling how long ago it had been sent and for the moment there was nothing I could do to help Hamlet until we saw if he returned, having made friends with the pirates, as I had advised.

Ever realised the seriousness of the situation with which I had become involved, even the receipt of such a letter could cost me my life. I persuaded Ever that for the moment the best option was to sit tight and do nothing about it.

CHAPTER 22

A melia was also worried about Ever being in my sphere of reality without appropriate clothing for Elizabethan London. Maddie was working hard to produce suitable garments, but was often on the verge of tears, as Spikey, the Practice cat, had deserted them. Indeed, he hadn't been seen since Ever and I had left. Amelia had written to me about Spikey, but had only received a note from me, asking who William Wayte might happen to be. There was no mention of the cat, because frankly, I hadn't read her note about it, but had just charged ahead, writing a new one about my own concerns. It was for Maddie, her last hope, that Spikey might have travelled with Ever and Amelia. I can understand that now, but at the time I was oblivious to the problem.

Things were not going well concerning the 'missing consulting room.' Mrs Prenderghast had rung Mr Smart to complain that the 'elusive room' had disappeared again and a rather officious letter, addressed to the Head of the Practice, had been received. The letter from Mr Smart was uncompromising. The district council planning department was launching an official investigation, with a view to prosecution, which could carry a substantial fine, plus an instruction to restore the room with a deadline set by them. That would cause major difficulties for me, enforcing my return before I had completed my mission. The Practice had just 24 hours to provide an explanation and an action plan to restore the consulting room to the building in which it was last seen.

Dafydd, meanwhile, desperate to find Spikey, in order to console Maddie, as well as to offset the problems being posed by Mr Smart, had put in a request for stress-related absence and permission to take Maddie to a rival practice for psychotherapeutic help over the missing cat! Amelia was furious. Psychotherapists in the competitive practice concerned were well-known Freudians, who if they found out about my mission, whilst Maddie was on the couch, would no doubt report the matter to the British Psychological Society, with a request for an investigation into our conduct. They would point out the dangers to my mind, in sending me out to a place, where I was determined to 'communicate with the dead.' Heaven knows what Maddie might have overheard in the conversations between the four of us at the Practice. She may reveal, for example, that I was living in a brothel, and had now taken my Ever with me to that resort. Additionally, there were the ethical considerations that might come under scrutiny, concerning our attempts to change history, which had caused tension even among the four of us. The problems seemed endless.

At least Amelia had taken some comfort in knowing that I had no financial, emotional or physical investment in George Wilkins' House of Pleasures – except for renting a room in which I could sleep. Fortunately, she didn't know that I had enjoyed the services of Dolly the Younger, for a night when I was feeling particularly down and required some revitalising stimulation. At that time, Ever didn't know about Dolly either. I wanted to leave that to one side for the present, except for the fact that I had put it down on expenses, as a claim labelled 'Sleeping Cordial: Dolly Mixture'. Amelia, when going through my expense claims, had sent a note back asking if it had done the trick, seeing as she was also finding it hard to sleep at night. If so, could I acquire a flagon of 'Dolly Mixture' for her when she next visited or when I came home? It was all building up to a perfect storm.

The first lightning strike was my request for information about William Wayte. Meticulous as ever, Amelia had found out that William Wayte in November 1596 apparently had Shakespeare 'bound over to keep the peace'. It came in an attachment addressed to the Sheriff of Surrey. Wayte had complained that he was in danger of life and limb, from William Shakespeare, Francis Langley, Dorothy Soaer and one other. Intrigued, Amelia had made investigations at the local library, where she was greeted by the librarian with a cheery,

"Hello, Doctor Angel, I've heard you've lost a consulting room again!"

This didn't do her nerves much good, but she found an appropriate book to discover that William Wayte was the stepson of William Gardiner, who was one of those complaining about the Blackfriars being reopened by its new owners, for theatrical productions.

Putting two and two together, she decided that Wayte must have got into an altercation of some kind with Shakespeare and maybe a fight had broken out. Possibly that was Wayte's intent as he wanted to damage Shakespeare as the poster boy for the Lord Chamberlain's Men, by making Will out to be a person of a volatile nature and unsavoury habits.

Amelia had gone further to find out about the others on the list, who were to be bound over. Dorothy Soaer was the owner of 'Soaer's Lets', in Paris Gardens and 'The Elephant', close to the Globe, (both of which I had been intending to visit in search of new rooms for Ever and me). She also appeared to be a 'madame' running brothels, which a business in which Francis Langley also had commercial interests. Indeed, he was in Amelia's words 'a Rachman type of profiteer' from his rented-out properties and he had a reputation for violence for which he had previously been hauled before the authorities.

All of this frightened Amelia. Why on earth was I wanting to know about Gardiner's stepson, William Wayte and his connection to Shakespeare? Was this the William Shakespeare with whom she had secretly corresponded? Surely such a person wouldn't be the same as the one that history had deified as a god of poetry and the theatre? But as she read more, she found out that Langley had actually also invested in theatre properties, including the Rose Theatre and more importantly the Blackfriars Theatre, in which Shakespeare's company had a financial interest.

It all sounded quite unsavoury, even to an experienced Psychotherapist such as herself. Not knowing why I had enquired about Wayte, she started to worry that Ever and I were perhaps getting ourselves into deep water. Amelia, therefore, summed it up as follows, in no particular order:

- Shakespeare might be an unsavoury character, getting into brawls;
- Alternatively, Shakespeare could be innocent, up from the country, being set up by Wayte and Gardiner his stepfather;
- Jacob is getting himself involved with a gang of brothel owners, villains and murderers (Amelia did have a tendency to be overdramatic at times);
- Jacob has Ever with him sleeping in a brothel;
- Jacob is still convinced that Shakespeare is 'just a front for the Company, a living logo or poster boy';
- Jacob isn't answering simple queries;
- The Practice is accused of having lost a consulting room;
- Dafydd is threatening to take leave for stress just at the time that we are expecting a visit from Mr

Smart, who is demanding to see the senior partner (herself);
- Ever needs Elizabethan clothes;
- Spikey is still missing!
- Maddie needs to find Spikey.

Having read over the list, Amelia sent me another message saying:

"Wayte dangerous; Smart causing trouble; consulting room needs to come back; Spikey missing. Abort mission."

CHAPTER 23

A melia's latest instruction to abort the mission must have arrived soon after Ever and I had left for the Globe Theatre. Ever had agreed with Augustine to help rehearse the cast, in what Ever termed 'the pansexual realities that are *As You Like It*.' Augustine didn't quite know what Ever meant by that phrase, nor frankly did I, but it sounded good, and who am I to question such erudition? Critics, after all, exalt in such phrases all the time, under the impression that we all know what they signify, and more importantly, the relationship of the signified to the signifier or vice versa, whatever that means! So why shouldn't a Psychotherapist, interested in the theatre, do the same?

What Augustine was needing, was help particularly with two new boy actors, who were addressing the female roles of Rosalind and Celia. Rosalind is a woman who dresses as a man and then pretends to be a woman in order to teach the man she fancies how to woo her. For some, it was a bit of a conundrum of a part for a young boy to conceive – perhaps that is an inappropriate word. Rather, let's say, by which to find the essence beneath the complexity of the Rosalind role.

How is he, a boy, able to express the yearning of a girl,

Rosalind? She is the daughter of a usurped Duke, (Duke Senior) who for her self-protection, dresses as a man and runs away from the traitorous, volatile usurper Duke Ferdinand. He has taken her father's office and title, whilst she, (disguised as a man), has the effrontery to take the said Duke Ferdinand's daughter, the willing Celia, who is her cousin, with her(him), into the forest of Arden.

Besides, how does the boy actor playing Celia, who is running away as a disguised country woman named Aliena, play his role as a girl, who has deceived her father because of her loyalty and love for Rosalind?

Rosalind, moreover, in dressing as a man, chooses to call herself Ganymede, which is a mythological name with homosexual connotations. Even more complicated, is that once in the forest, where they take refuge, Ganymede then pretends to be Rosalind, (who she is) in order to teach Orlando, the son of a now-deceased enemy of her uncle (the usurping Duke Ferdinand) how to woo 'him' (Ganymede) as if he were Rosalind because in the story, he is she! Orlando, incidentally, has also fled to the forest, with an agèd servant named Adam, for fear of being murdered by his brother Oliver.

No wonder the play is called *As You Like It*, as these nonsensical convolutions take some 'liking' to be understood. Yet it seems to work when acted well and to act it well the newly recruited boys apparently needed some help from someone interested in dual sexual identities and attraction, namely Ever.

These were the boys, who were to take over the roles from those who had originally played them. The latter had found themselves in some trouble. They, in the first performances, had acted so well as boys playing girls, or in one case a boy pretending to be a girl pretending to be a young man, that they had stirred up the male libido in the audience. This had resulted in the boy actors concerned having to be guarded by some of the adult actors, on their way home, in order to prevent them from being attacked and indecently assaulted, by seriously sexually worked up spectators.

It was all rather unfortunate. Augustine blamed, in particular, the play's epilogue. This had been delivered by the rather beautiful boy playing the first Rosalind, who proved to be a little too flirtatious with the final lines,

> If I were a woman, I would kiss as many of you as had beards that pleased me, complexions that liked me and breaths that I defied not. And I am sure, as many as have good beards or good faces or sweet breaths will, for my kind offer, when I make curtsy, bid me farewell.

Something of a riot broke out when male testosterone levels, already raised by the play, rose exponentially, leading to an invasion of the stage.

The success and notoriety of the production brought in the money, of course, as many performances took place before the audience numbers started to tumble, due to the competition from the private theatres and the ever-present moral outrage of the Puritan anti-theatre brigade. This helped to force the company to tour with the play, to gain extra funds.

Augustine, who had exempted himself from the tour, was determined to revive the play at the Globe with a new cast of boys, some of whom, I gathered, had been 'pressed' into joining the company. Kidnapping boy actors was not uncommon, and I was discovering that the theatre wasn't the purest of professions. There were big sums of money involved, and the financiers, were often salubrious characters.

Ever felt, however, that it would be possible to do a rehearsal or two and Augustine was ready to pay. I went along to give some moral support as Ever started work.

Frankly, the young boys looked at Ever like someone who had come from the moon. Ever was somewhat colourfully dressed as there hadn't been any Elizabethan clothing available and Ever's dress sense, at home, had always been extravagant. The theatre is the home of eccentricities and the cast, after the initial shock, seemed to take to Ever's exuberance and humour. To be fair, Ever played to these idiosyncrasies – as some might call them – because they, I have to say, are the persona of Ever that attracts us all.

"Now don't think I am so strange that I can't help you with this wonderful play"' Ever began, going on to explain. "But I come from far, far away, where if you don't wish to be known as a man or a woman, you don't have to agree to be a man or a woman. You can be what you want to be: binary, non-binary, transgender, pangender, dual-gender, asexual, heterosexual, homosexual, gender non-specific, or other varieties of definitions that come in and out as your, psychology, biology, dictate. You see, you don't have to be stereotyped by what people want you to be. Indeed, I see this play as being very modern. Its outrageous title *As You Like It* encompasses freedom of modernity and expression, for you my darlings – Oh please," Ever laughed, "excuse that expression, but you look so innocently beautiful that I feel at home already. Now, who is the child destined for this pansexual acting experience: a boy, 'a codling when 'tis almost an apple,' who is to play the role of Rosalind, a young woman, who falls in love with a young man whose name is Orlando - how sweet is that?"

A young boy stood up and introduced himself as Harry.

"Ah Harry," Ever gushed, walking around him, surveying him from back to front and head to toe, "You are perfect. Now listen to me. Your father was a Duke, called Senior, probably because the scribbler of the role couldn't think what to name him." Ever paused, before saying, with a questioning glance in my direction, "The scribbler can be forgiven for that since such is the mind of a genius. Duke Senior has been usurped by his brother Frederick, who became Duke, which was clearly not a brotherly thing to do. It wasn't nice. It was wilful, inconsiderate and unlawful. So much so that your father had to flee for his life into the forest of Arden, but you remained at the new Duke's court, because his unfortunate child, your cousin Celia, begged that you might be allowed to do so." Ever, with closed eyes, said, "Meditate on this fact my dear, since it was such a brave, lovely thing for your cousin to do."

Suddenly Ever looked around saying, "And where is Celia? Come here my little one."

Somewhat afeared, another boy left his seat, to be enveloped gently by Ever, "You are the daughter of that nasty usurping Duke Frederick, which of course, is a hard fact to bear, but in compensation, you are the dear cousin and friend of Rosalind, whom you love deeply."

It was at this point that I decided it was time to go in search of my new lodgings, as I had previously arranged. I left Ever in full flow, identifying the actors Orlando and his cruel brother Oliver. What Ever was going to make of the two characters named Jaques and Jaques in the play, I didn't wish to know, but as I exited the theatre, I could hear Ever proclaiming, with a touch of sad melancholy, that, "All the world's a stage / And all the men and women merely players / They have their exits and their entrances / And one man in his time plays many parts,/ His acts being seven ages."

I laughed to myself at the ironies which were besetting the two of us, and I went on my way.

CHAPTER 24

My destination was the 'Elephant', a short walk away from the Globe on the corner of Horseshoe alley, near the riverbank. There I was hoping to find new lodgings, although my mind was still filled with the sexual complexities of *As You Like It* that Ever was clarifying to help the boys with their performance. Augustine had told me that the 'Elephant' had once been a brothel but was now a place where many of the actors resided, and I half wondered whether it might be where I'd find some evidence of the elusive Mr Shakespeare. I'd often seen the place, with its sign of a painted elephant over the door, but not knowing what I'd find inside, I had never entered. There was a breeze coming off the river, which carried its customary stench. I suppose people, having lived in London most of their lives, had become so accustomed to it, that they hardly noticed it. I found it repugnant and therefore, even as I approached the hostel, I had significant misgivings that it would be the right place for Ever and me to stay.

The manager, Richard Wisely, proved a pleasant enough man. I had always thought Wilkins to be rather 'shifty' but Richard seemed very straightforward. The house itself was comfortable, by Elizabethan standards, with tapestried curtains at the unglazed windows, and around the beds, in some but not all of the rooms. There was a kitchen area and a place a little like a tavern servery, where you could eat and drink. If it hadn't been for the awful smell, I may have been attracted to it. One of the rooms I saw, looked across the Thames towards the old St Paul's, where I had seen the Marston play in the cloistered area, which formed the theatre. Not far from the Cathedral, though I couldn't exactly say where, was the site of one of the first playhouses, to be built in London. This was in Shoreditch, built by James Burbage and called The Theatre. It was where the Lord Chamberlain's Men formerly had their home. William Shakespeare, it was said, had rooms overlooking St Helen's Parish Church within walking distance from the playhouse. But to my mind, this was all part of the fiction of his creation. It was recorded that the rooms he hired were owned by the worshipful company of leather sellers. This cleverly helped to give a false veracity to the identity of Shakespeare the dramatist, since a certain 'William Shakespeare' who was said to live there, had a father named John, who was the Bailiff of Stratford and who happened to own a leather business. This John Shakespeare had notoriously got himself into trouble over financial irregularities in the sheep trade, as well as claims that he refused to give up the old papist religion.

There was no doubt that such a family called Shakespeare existed. The question was, whether this country boy William, who had left school at fourteen, could have been educated enough to have written plays and poems. To my mind, he was no more than a symbol such as Hercules carrying his Globe. He may not have even known how his name was being exploited.

I knew, of course, the story of the Lord Chamberlain's Men, who had had difficulties with Giles Allen, the owner of the land north of the Thames, on which 'The Theatre' had been built. He had refused to extend the lease, so the company dismantled the playhouse and transported the wood and other materials over the river and built a new theatre, the Globe, in Maiden Lane, just a hundred yards away from where I was standing.

I asked Richard whether any of the actors stayed with him when they were rebuilding the new playhouse on this side of the river. He said that they had and continued to do so, although some of them were away touring at present. Richard was a very open kind of man, ready to chat, so he went on to tell me how, one night, he had helped the men to unload their wood for the Globe, as they brought their barges across the river. He had put lights in all the windows of the Elephant, to direct them to the appropriate spot on the south bank, and then went out to help them to land their cargo. His young son, Sam, meanwhile, tended the lights so that they wouldn't burn out. It was all hard work but there was plenty of laughter and good humour.

He had commented that he knew who I was and that I wore the Queen's Colours, but he wondered how I had built my strangely clad workroom overnight, without anyone helping or knowing. He then took me by surprise by asking me outright, whether I was some kind of informer for the Government. Apparently, there was a rumour that I was spying on illegal trading that was occurring up and down the river. Maybe that was why he thought I needed rooms with windows facing the Thames. He didn't mind if that was going to be the case, as long as I could pay the rent. With that, his eye twitched, a wink, in the same manner as I'd noticed with Augustine. I laughed and said it was nonsense, what else was there for me to say? But I did make some comment about the way rumours begin and are sustained.

I thought to myself, that it was by such falsehoods, that the Elizabethan Government existed, weaving the rumours like spiders' webs. I wondered if the playwrights, Christopher Marlowe and Thomas Kyd, had been slandered in such a way, before dying within a year of each other in 1593 and 1594.

Maybe something similar was behind the falsehood of Shakespeare's name. This glove maker's son from Stratford was perhaps a front because as a dramatist he didn't exist. He was a name taken out of a hat, so to speak, a traveller, who on his father's business had once taken lodgings in St Helen's Parish, not far from The Theatre, which he may have frequented. He could have been a stranger, who had come to London, like the Pedant, who is paid to counterfeit Vincentio, in *The Taming of the Shrew.* This was a play written about the same time that this Shakespeare character from Stratford happened to visit London on the first occasion. That was it! I had worked out the scam. The company had even placed something like it in a play. It is the kind of thing that artists do all the time. But was Richard Wisely in on their act? So, I asked him outright, if one of the actors named William Shakespeare, had ever taken lodgings with him. As I expected, he didn't flinch. He said that he had heard of the actor but had never met him.

"Isn't he the writer of their plays?" I interrogated.

"I wouldn't know," he replied. "As I have never met him, I wouldn't really know."

"I thought he was one of the actors, as well as a writer. I presumed he was one of those who floated the dismantled old theatre across the river, the night you helped them." I prompted.

"No, I don't recall," Richard said with a twitch of the eye. "As I say, I've heard of him but I've never met him."

We looked at each other suspiciously, but the eye didn't twitch again. I decided to make one last attempt. "But haven't you seen William Shakespeare acting on the stage?"

"I might have done," he said. "But I can't remember all their names. I certainly know Richard Burbage, who is a really nice man. He doesn't stay here, but he has popped in a few times to see some of our tenants."

I wasn't getting anywhere and couldn't decide whether he was telling the truth or not. I told him with regret, that I wouldn't be able to take the room as it was too close to the river, and that my 'wife' had a weak chest. He said he was sorry but maybe I'd like to try 'Soares Rents' by the bowling alley in Paris Garden Lane, where actors sometimes stayed. I wondered whether he now thought that my job was to spy on the actors. As I left, I decided to have one last try.

"Do you think that Will Shakespeare might have lodgings in 'Soaers Rents'?" He laughed and repeated that he didn't know the man and couldn't enlighten me any further. I don't know if I wanted his eye to twitch or not, but it didn't and I took my leave.

CHAPTER 25

I arrived back at the Globe just as Ever was starting to wind up the rehearsal. She asked the boys what they had made of the play. The perception of those playing Rosalind and Celia, in particular, made a deep impact on me.

"I suppose," Boy Celia said, "that the play tells us that we all tend to dress up and pretend to be something we might be, rather than just be what we are. But in the pretending, we are revealing what we really are, through the roles we play."

Boy Rosalind agreed, arguing that in life, we are constantly pretending, often being someone that we are not, in order to get what we want. It is a kind of hypocrisy, operating at all levels.

This boy actor continued, "We even sometimes hide away so as not to show ourselves to others. That's why in the play, we run into the wood, a kind of madness, through which we work out, who we love and, in my case, how I can encourage someone in their love for me." Ever praised them but asked what happens if, when you run away, you find that the person you think you love, is not the one that you really love but someone else, irrespective of whether they are a boy or a girl. Does it matter? The boy was quick to understand that he, as

Rosalind dressed as young man Ganymede, had to pretend to be a woman, in order to teach Orlando how to love.

"And yet," he said, "I am a boy and everyone knows that to be the case."

I couldn't help interrupting,

"Yes," I said. "But everyone knows that this is just a play and not real life!" I looked at Ever questioningly, but it was boy Rosalind who answered.

"I agree," he said. "But what if it were? Isn't that what theatre is all about?" I laughed and Ever said that we needed to go, but would return to take them through another rehearsal later in the week. Augustine was looking at the two of us thoughtfully, but boy Celia broke his gaze by giving Ever a hug, and boy Rosalind did the same.

Back in our consulting room, Ever and I agreed about the perception of the boys. Ever had enjoyed working with them. I, of course, was dealing with a different play, *Hamlet*, where a King and Chief Minister, in their ambition and self-importance, create fictions of reality, which the theatre needed to uncover.

In our adventure, we were dealing with so many levels of perception that we had almost lost the understanding of what was true. The deaths I had seen through plague, disease and execution were real enough in the Virtual World which we had entered. But didn't they also reflect things that historically had once happened? Hamlet was running away into feigned or self-constructed madness as we run away into the fiction we create, experience and enjoy whatever the emotion it engenders.

I asked Ever, "Is it true that you love me?"

Ever paused before replying, "That is a difficult question. What is love?"

I replied, "What is truth?"

Neither of us was ready to answer such questions about ourselves so we talked about *Hamlet* and how the play might be reflecting life under an Elizabethan Government. For example,

Polonius could be seen as Elizabeth's Chief Minister, Robert Cecil, who was responsible for arranging the imprisonment and death of many people. Also, we discussed how the power of monarchs and politicians of any era can abuse power. How easy it was for Claudius to send the Prince away and callously arrange his execution. How, with equal callousness, could Hamlet himself rearrange for Rosencrantz and Guildenstern to be executed in his stead? How could Henry Vlll easily dispose of various wives and politicians, including his chancellor? How in our day, could the president of a great foreign power, have one of his own former spies executed in an English cathedral city? The world which I had left was one of fake news, in which the lies and deceits of politicians had become common place, but I realised that this wasn't anything new.

We had started to talk about whether Hamlet was truly in love, when, as the gods might have it, there was a knock at the door. I opened it and there stood a distraught Hamlet,

"Ophelia is dead."

"Ophelia?"

"Dead!"

CHAPTER 26

Back home, Jackie was restless. Amelia, however, had always appeared to be organised and on top of all the aspects of the experiment. She was worried, of course, that I was getting drawn into the William Wayte circle with his nefarious friends and that I had not responded to her instruction to abort the mission. But I had neglected to check my messages. As I was later to learn, Jackie wasn't concerned so much about Wayte, but the fact was, she was missing Ever whom she was longing to see again. She was even secretly planning to come out to visit us both. If I had known this, perhaps matters would not have turned out the way that they did.

As it was, in my Virtual World, I was facing Hamlet in distress, who, as he was about to enter my room, saw Ever, a stranger, sitting in 'his' chair. He looked at Ever, then back at me. He abruptly apologised, thinking that I had another client and rushed away. I ran after him but lost him in the narrow streets. I returned to Ever, who had seen and heard what had happened. I was all for trying to find him at the theatre. But Ever persuaded me to wait, since I needed to be in the consulting room if he returned.

I explained to Ever over tea, that the lodgings at the Elephant were unsuitable and that we needed to go elsewhere to find some. But there was something else on my mind. So many things had been said, or more importantly not said, about William Shakespeare, that I needed to sort the fact from the fiction. I wanted, therefore, to go to Stratford, to find out whether this son of a leather seller and wool merchant, who had once lived in St Helen's Parish, was the man being used to front the theatre company. Ever pedantically corrected me. Surely, I meant 'was the man who was being used to front the company, or as tradition has it, the man who wrote the plays.'

I pointed out that we could get horses and ride there, staying overnight at Marlow, Oxford and Shipston, crossing the Avon into Stratford within four days. There could be no proof one way or another about whether Shakespeare was the dramatist until we had talked to the man of that name who lived in Stratford.

Also, at some point, the two of us needed to go home. I was getting tired of the smell, the deaths in the streets and I was aware that the plague would get worse over the next few months and I didn't want to be around at that time.

"Why?" Ever asked.

"We know that in February 1603 the Queen will die. If we are here then, we will immediately lose the protection I have, as up until now I have been wearing the Queen's Colours."

Ever suggested that we would just have to get the King's Colours. We knew, of course, that it would be King James, and that he would bestow patronage by making the Lord Chamberlain's Men into the King's Men. We also knew that if we stayed on until the queen died, we would be in London during one of the most virulent outbreaks of the plague. Even the new King, coming down from Scotland, wouldn't enter the city, but would camp outside until it was safe to enter.

Ever commented ruefully, that we should be used to such conditions, as during the Covid-19 pandemic, we had had to stay shut away in our houses and then we had had to wear masks when we eventually went out.

There was, however, another issue on my mind that we needed to take into account. If Hamlet were to die soon, which looked likely, our main source of income would dry up and we'd need to come home anyway. Ever looked at me in dismay. "How can you talk about Hamlet just in terms of the income he brings you? You have a responsibility as his Psychotherapist, to look after your client and that overrides any other consideration. Just a while ago, the Prince left your door in a state of grief over the death of his girlfriend, and now you are thinking of leaving him to fend for himself, just as he is facing the most difficult crisis of his life."

Ever was rightly very angry with me, crossing over to the window and staring out silently.

I tried to play things down but Ever was extremely annoyed.

"I just can't believe that you are Jackie's brother. She'd have never been so selfish or so obsessive. Her first concern would have been for the Prince. Yours is with this bee in your bonnet that you have about the identity of Shakespeare. Does it matter a damn who wrote the plays? I'm going back to the theatre. I'll see you later." With that Ever walked out of the door, shutting it firmly!

CHAPTER 27

As is often the case with arguments, the one between Ever and me over Hamlet had a deeper significance than its apparent cause. Coming into the Virtual World with me was bound to be a test of our relationship. I thought to myself that Ever was happier working at the theatre with the boys, pretending to be girls, than Ever was with me. From my point of view, I was beginning to question my love for Ever. In addition to that, however, I had become more obsessed with the Shakespeare element of my mission and becoming aware that I was failing in my responsibility as a Psychotherapist to my client.

I was, of course, concerned about the Prince, but in the emotional state of grief, which he had shown at the door, I wasn't worried that now was the time he might kill himself, or fail to stop himself from being killed. People on the verge of suicide often reach a plateau of calm, once they have made the decision to do the deed. That resolve settles them, often giving false comfort to their family and friends, who mistakenly think it a signal of some form of recovery. If Hamlet had been calm, I would have been worried, but he was not. He could still have an accident, being so deeply in grief and emotionally disturbed, but I was more confident at this point, that he would not end it all by his own hand than I had been in some of my earlier sessions with him.

As I was writing my notes and feeling somewhat sorry for myself over the argument with Ever, I became aware that I was being watched. Perhaps a shadow had come across the room, or perhaps I heard something. I looked to the window and there staring at me was Hamlet. I signalled to him and I shouted that I was on my own and we could talk.

Dishevelled, and with eyes red with weeping, Hamlet entered the room and took his customary seat. I boiled some water for tea.

"Who was that with you?" He asked.

"Doctor Ever Truslove." I replied, "One of the partners in my Practice, *4 Psychotherapists 4 U*. He looked at me as I was pouring the water into the mugs. I was going to add that Ever had come out to join me because we were in love, but something stopped me from saying it.

I gave him his tea and sat down opposite with one for myself. He took one sip and set it aside. He sighed and rubbed his face and brow with his hands, until finally, with his eyes covered by his fingers, he just sat in silence, as if his mind was going over and over all that had happened.

I waited for him to tell me about Ophelia, but everything appeared too much for him. He started to fidget in his chair, before standing up, going to the window and going back to the chair.

He looked at me with despairing eyes. Eventually he began,

"It was all my fault, I killed her father, fled, was caught by Claudius, sent abroad with my so-called friends who were going to take me to my death. I never gave her a thought. I sorted out Rosencrantz and Guildenstern, who by now are likely to be dead, but so is she. My Ophelia has gone. She can't come back"

He told me that he had found out, that whilst he was away, she had lost her wits. With the death of his father King Hamlet, he had played at insanity, but she had actually gone insane with the death of hers. She had interrupted Claudius who, with her brother Laertes, was plotting how to avenge her father's death. She gave flowers and herbs to Claudius, Gertrude and to her brother, whom she didn't recognise, or if she did, it was all confused in her grief-torn mind.

Hamlet regretted that he hadn't been there to help her, but he regretted more, that he was as responsible for this madness of hers as he was for the death of her father. How could such a one as he, do such deeds?

Apparently, she had climbed out onto a branch which overhung the river. It had given way and she had fallen. The water enveloped her clothes and pulled her down. So it was that she drowned. In her madness, she had killed herself. The priest declared that the death was 'doubtful'; that it may have been deliberate and so they buried her with little Christian ceremony, with the clowns and commoners of this world.

I waited for Hamlet to continue, but after a moment or two, I told him that it certainly was not suicide. Her mind was deranged and she would not have known that the branch was unsafe, or her garments unsuitable. I commented that clerics can be as pharisaic today as they were at the time of Jesus, and he should pay no heed to their rulings when so many of them misunderstood the nature of the world.

He nodded his agreement but kept going back to the fact that he had killed Polonius, telling me the story again. Just as the Friar, whom I had helped by accident, kept telling me about his guilt at running away from Juliet's tomb, so Hamlet had become obsessed by his murder of the Chief Minister, which he insisted, over and over again, had led to the death of Ophelia, whom he professed to have loved.

As a Psychotherapist with problems of my own, I was having to deal with so many of his issues simultaneously: the death of his father; the haunting by the Ghost; his accusation of his mother's incest; his feigned madness; his plotting against

Claudius; his introspection; his killing of Polonius; his capture and escape; his obsession with death. I recalled that someone once remarked that Hamlet's emotions were in 'excess of the facts as they appeared'. But analysing him, I could not agree. From the beginning, the facts of his situation had escalated to a point that whilst he attempted to show an outward sign of control, his mind continued to conjure images of death and culpability.

He told me that he had come across the gravedigger happily singing at his work. He had engaged the man in conversation about the grave that was being prepared. The labourer was nonchalant and answered in a matter-of-fact way, about death, throwing up stinking old skulls from the grave. They could have been anybody's remains because that is the state in which death leaves us all. One of them turned out to be a jester called Yorick, whom Hamlet had known. But it could have been anyone, even a great leader such as Alexander the Great or Julius Caesar. Everyone dies. When Hamlet had questioned the grave digger, the man had told him that it takes eight years, maybe nine for the body to rot. It was then that he saw Claudius, Gertrude and Laertes coming to the grave with a body, which turned out to be that of Ophelia.

He became thoughtful again, muttering over and over that he had wanted it to be Claudius who had died, not Ophelia. It wasn't. All that had happened had been his fault, even his pretended madness had made him 'mad'.

In front of me I could see in Hamlet, an example of the fine line that exists between imagining and doing, pretence and actuality, fiction and reality: the Virtual World created in the mind and the world into which we are born.

The interaction of relationships between the one world and the other, between the pretending and the doing, is such that violence may be inflicted, not on oneself, but accidentally on others. In my view, he was 'the fault' but it wasn't 'his fault'. He was mentally disturbed. The circumstances had dictated an action, which in his state, he had instinctively taken, when he killed Polonius, thinking him to be the King. The ramifications of his actions, like a stone thrown into a pond, had rippled outwards to engulf Ophelia. But where had they all started? I asked him if it had been with him seeing the Ghost, but he denied that emphatically.

He thought for some time, before asking me if I thought it was because of the sudden and unexplained death of his 'supposed' father. I said that this was something we might consider during our next session. I told him that he needed to take time and that I needed to go elsewhere. It would be another two weeks before I could see him again, but that if he needed to see someone during that time, my colleague Doctor Truslove, would be here and he could talk to Ever as easily as he talked to me.

I had, in saying that, determined that Ever would not accompany me to meet Mr Shakespeare in Stratford, but I felt that I had also shown my care to the Prince.

In taking his leave of me, he gave me money for the session. I was grateful because I would be able to use this for any expenses, whilst I was away.

CHAPTER 28

If tensions were developing between Ever and myself at this time, there was also a growing tension at home between Jackie and Amelia. Amelia refused to entertain the idea that Jackie should go to Elizabethan England, but Jackie was fed up of being on the side-lines. She was the only one not to have travelled into the Virtual World in order to experience life there. Amelia understood this, but they had a Practice to run and they also had to sort out the Prenderghast – Smart problem. Amelia, at this point, did not realise that Jackie had an ulterior motive – she desperately wanted to see Ever. Their words of affection, which I had overheard on my brief but eventful return, were not superficial, whatever my Ever might have protested. It is said that where there is love, there is a way, and that came with Ever's urgent request to Maddie, for some clothes more appropriate for life in Elizabethan London. Ever also told Dafydd that I couldn't live in the same clothes all the time and so Maddie had decided to tailor another set for me at the Practice's expense. The two sets of clothes were in Dafydd's office, waiting for Amelia to decide on the method of transportation.

Whether Amelia liked it or not, Jackie was determined that

she was going to bring them to us. At first, she had to work out exactly how she was going to enter the Virtual World, so she started to stay late at night at the Practice, using the master key to enter Amelia's room and the password, (16CoRamBis03) to access Amelia's confidential files. The risk was that Amelia would find out because of 'last seen date'. But why would Amelia be wanting to look at these notes during the next few days? When she did it would be too late.

Concerned for her own safety as a woman travelling out into an unknown land, a Shakespearean forest of uncertainty, she planned to dress in the male clothes that Maddie had made for me. That way she would feel safer, if, for example, she became lost, as people would think she were me. The only thing that she did not possess was the Queen's Colours, but, of course, she knew nothing about them, and the protection they afforded me.

Ever, after our argument, had taken another successful rehearsal of *As You Like It*. When Ever returned to the lodgings, I said that Hamlet had been for his latest session and had left in a calmer state than I had seen him for some time. We had arranged that we would meet again in two weeks.

"So, you have manipulated for yourself, some time to go to Stratford?" Ever sneered. I didn't rise to the bait, because frankly, I knew that what Ever said was true.

"You are probably right," I admitted resignedly. "Because that is what I am intending to do."

Ever looked at me with disdain. I wanted Ever to understand that I had a dual mission to fulfil and for me, the one was as important as the other. I needed to get to Stratford before our return to the Real World.

"What does it matter if the dramatist is a marketing front?" Ever said exasperatedly. "We have the plays and the poems. That's all that matters. But if you want, you go on your search to prove your ridiculous theory and desert your client in doing so, but I'm staying here."

I felt relieved at first, even triumphant, as this was precisely what I had wanted her to say, and which I had told Hamlet she would do. But in retrospect, I realised that my obsession, rather than my concern for others, was driving me in a way that was unprofessional and which I have since tried to avoid. Nevertheless, at that time I confirmed rather patronisingly that Ever was right and would be better off remaining in London. Ever's scowl caused me to regret my words so I quickly suggested that we should go to the tavern for some food.

As we walked the short distance to Wilkins' Tavern, from the consulting room, in brooding silence, I realised something of what I had done. For me to leave London, was to put Ever in danger. I couldn't leave Ever alone. In my stupidity, I had told Hamlet that he could see Ever if needed, but I hadn't mentioned that yet to Ever. The whole row between us was something I had constructed, not just because of my mission, - to hell with my mission - it was because since Ever had come to join me, I had realised that we were not in love with each other. I had also felt betrayed by my twin sister Jackie.

Ever, meanwhile, was mulling things over and was simmering.

"What happens?" Ever asked as we found somewhere to sit in the tavern, "if Hamlet does need you?"

"I thought," I replied, "He might be able to have a session with you."

"You thought what?" Ever exclaimed, "I suppose you told him that!"

"Yes, I did as it happens."

"Well thank you!" Ever vehemently replied," adding, "I am not hungry, I am off to bed."

With that, Ever got up from the table and went to our room. Augustine was in the tavern watching us. He caught my eye and signalled to me not to follow. He then came across to join me.

"You both need to calm down." He said in a caring way. "And give yourselves some time."

Augustine asked me what was going on and I said that I wanted to meet with Shakespeare and was frustrated that I couldn't. I knew that I would soon be needed back home for other duties. So, I was proposing to go to Stratford to try and find him. Augustine gave me a hard look. I waited. Was this the moment that he was going to deny Shakespeare's authorship and tell me the truth? At last, with a cough, he said,

"We are a little concerned at the moment about where Will might be."

"What do you mean?" I asked eagerly. "You said that he was in the country. So, I presume this meant at his home in Warwickshire."

"It may be that he is in Warwickshire." Augustine said enigmatically, "but likewise, it may be that he is in Wiltshire."

"Where in Wiltshire?" I asked with some dismay.

"At Wilton House, the home of William Herbert, the Earl of Pembroke."

We looked at each other suspiciously. I had instantly recognised the name William Herbert as the possible identity of Mr W H, to whom the poet 'William Shakespeare' in 1609, was to dedicate his Sonnet sequence of a predominantly homosexual nature. In the autumn of 1602, the year in which we were talking, such revelations as made in the Sonnets, could in practice have resulted in execution. I thought that I should press to find out more.

"Why would Shakespeare be at the Earl of Pembroke's home?" I asked innocently.

"I don't know that he is there," Augustine prevaricated, "He just might be."

"But why?" I insisted.

"Because he and William are good friends and Will quite often goes there. The Earl likes him. They sometimes meet at his house, or sometimes in Oxford, as the Earl is fond of the University."

Augustine was being cautious with his words and yet was leading me on. So, I stopped beating around the bush.

"Do you mean, the William Herbert, about whom some scurrilous sonnets have been privately circulating in London?"

Augustine looked at me uncertainly and expressed the hope that it was from a private source that I had heard such things. He asked for an assurance that if so, I wouldn't in my capacity as someone with ties to the Government by wearing the Queen's Colours, talk about those poems in public. I, of course, assured him that I wouldn't.

My mind was darting from one matter to another since this overt revelation by Augustine was causing me a new problem. Was he deliberately putting me off the scent, distracting me from discovering the conspiracy? If I went to Stratford and Will wasn't there, it could be because he was miles away at Wilton House. If I went to the Earl of Pembroke's home, and Shakespeare wasn't there, it could be because he was in Stratford. But in any case, how would I, an unknown black man, even with the Queen's Colours, get admission to an aristocratic house? It could all be what we now call, a Catch 22, neatly being played by Augustine. Of course, Ever, back in the lodgings would say, that whatever it was, Augustine had now implied that Shakespeare, the dramatist, existed. But I wasn't going to be put off.

I determined that I was going to try my luck and go and find Will. Augustine protested that Will would be back in London very soon, but hinted that if I wanted to meet him sooner, I'd be advised to go to Wiltshire. To my mind, that meant that where I needed to go was Stratford. There I would find a William Shakespeare, without any problem. He would turn out to be a businessman in the leather and wool trade and certainly not a dramatist. I, of course, told Augustine the opposite. I said that I would go to find Will in Wiltshire, if they would let a black man into the Earl's great house.

Augustine assured me that the Queen's Colours would be enough, but nevertheless that he would write a note of introduction for me. I asked if he would also do one for Stratford, just in case I changed my mind. He agreed and then made a very generous offer. If Ever wished to stay in London to help with the rehearsals, lodgings at his home could be made available whilst I was away. His wife would be delighted to have Ever around and the house was in walking distance from the theatre. They could go in to work together, without any fear.

I thought that to be a very kind gesture. On hearing this later, Ever readily agreed and was even excited at the prospect of living with an Elizabethan family, but Ever insisted on spending some time in the consulting room, in case Hamlet returned.

I, therefore, made arrangements to hire relay horses from George Wilkins, picking up fresh animals at the taverns where he recommended me to stay. Everything was organised. I would start my journey to Stratford, and Ever would lodge with Augustine. I had thought of everything – or at least I thought I had.

CHAPTER 29

My route to Stratford took me along the river Thames towards the town of Marlow, where I was to stay overnight. What amazed me was the quietness of the countryside as I left the city and followed a surprisingly well-trodden bridleway through the fields and luscious woodland with the river sparkling not far away. The sky was a crystal blue and the air so fresh, in contrast to the stench of London and the pollution of my own time. There was the gentle sound of birdsong and a buzz of bees who were visiting the wild flowers peppering the undulating landscape. These provided a mixed scent, which in my own world I had not experienced even in a botanical garden. It was what a later poet, William Blake was to call 'England's green and pleasant land', but about which, our dramatist wrote;

I know a bank where the wild thyme blows,
Where oxlips and the nodding violet grows,
Quite overcanopied with luscious woodbine'
With sweet musk-roses, and with eglantine.

I noted that I had started to think of Shakespeare as 'our

dramatist'. The freedom of the countryside, away from the hard economics of the city, strangely made my theory of 'Shakespeare' being just a marketing ploy, seem far less credible. I felt that I had been released from the stifling capitalism that enveloped the world of theatre in the time of Elizabeth l and centuries later, in the reign of Elizabeth ll. Theatres in both ages had to fight for their existence, not only because of competition and political pressure, but also the economic hardship felt through the ravages of plague and pandemic. Here, looking at the landscape, I felt I could breathe and I understood how a man of creative sensitivity could be inspired.

Were my certainties fracturing in the absolute beauty of this ride, which even so close to the city, prompted thoughts of poetry and exquisite fantasy? I was unsure, not of my geographical bearings, but my mental ones. A friend, who had a little daughter, told me that once when she was playing deep in her fantasy world, she quite suddenly asked her mother,

"I am real, aren't I? I'm not pretend!"

Her mother, giving her a kiss, told her that she was not pretend. The little girl went happily back, into the imaginative world, which in play was so real.

As I rode along, I recalled the fantasy of *A Midsummer Night's Dream* in which lovers flee into a forest, not dissimilar to the one through which I was riding, in order to sort out their romantic problems. The story is set in Athens and in a nearby wood. Egeus, the father of Hermia appeals to Duke Theseus to make Hermia marry the man of his choice, Demetrius. However, she has refused as she is in love with Lysander. Her friend Helena loves Demetrius but he, having once loved her, has now settled on Hermia and is intent on marrying her, in line with her father's wishes.

The Duke himself is soon to marry Hippolyta, the Queen of the Amazons, whom he has defeated in battle. Duke Theseus rules that Hermia should obey her father and marry Demetrius, on pain of death or confinement to a convent. Hermia tells her friend Helena that she is intending to run away with Lysander. Helena, hoping to gain favour with Demetrius, reveals the plan to him. Demetrius pursues Hermia and Lysander into a wood and Helena follows him.

In the wood Oberon, the King of the Fairies has quarrelled with Titania, the Queen of the Fairies, over an Indian changeling boy, whom he wishes her to give to him as his page. She has refused and in order to punish her, Oberon instructs his servant sprite, Robin Goodfellow, known as Puck, to apply a love potion, derived from a flower, to the eyes of the sleeping Titania. This will make her fall in love with the first person she sees when she wakes up.

Noticing Demetrius and Helena at odds with each other, he also instructs the mischievous Puck to apply the potion to the eyes of Demetrius, while he is sleeping close to her. Puck mistakenly applies the potion to the eyes of Lysander, who on wakening sees Helena and falls in love with her. He pursues her instead of Hermia. Helena, however, is furious because she thinks that Lysander is making fun of her. Puck, on being told to right the wrong, then applies the potion to the eyes of Demetrius, who waking, also falls in love with Helena. Chaos ensues, as Hermia, now loved by neither man, quarrels with Helena, whilst the boys fight with each other over her.

Meanwhile, Puck, on seeing some workmen rehearsing a play in the wood, which they wish to present to Duke Theseus at his forthcoming marriage to Hippolyta, decides to play a trick on one of the actors. He endows Bottom, a weaver, with an ass' head. Titania, on waking, sees the transformed Bottom and falls in love with the ass. Confusion reigns, but an antidote is applied to allow Lysander to love Hermia again, whilst Demetrius remains in love with Helena. They are awoken in the wood, by the Duke, who is out hunting. Titania and Bottom, now released from his ass' head, return to their true selves. Bottom makes his way back into Athens, where, meeting up with his friends, they are chosen to perform their play for the

Duke and his bride. Meanwhile, in Fairyland, Titania, gives up her changeling boy to Oberon.

After the worker's performance of the strangely titled but hilarious play the 'mirthful tragedy of Pyramus and Thisbe', the contented lovers go to bed, whilst Oberon and Titania, now reconciled, together with their fairies, enter the palace to bless all within with a song.

This done, Puck is left alone on the stage to present an epilogue, so famous that I could recite it out loud as I went along.

If we shadows have offended,
Think but this and all is mended.
That you have but slumbered here
While these visions did appear,
And this weak and idle theme,
No more yielding but a dream,
Gentles do not reprehend.
If you pardon we will mend.
And, as I am an honest Puck,
If we have unearned luck,
Now to 'scape the serpent's tongue,
We will make amends ere long:
Else the Puck a liar call.
So, goodnight unto you all.
Give me your hands if we be friends,
And Robin shall restore amends.

The comedy rolled round in my mind as I was nearing my destination. In particular, I had thought of the conversation between the four lovers. When they are reconciled to each other, having been woken from their sleep in the forest by the Duke on his hunt, Demetrius, only half awake, says,

These things seem small and undistinguishable,

Like far off mountains turned into clouds

And Hermia replies,

Methinks I see things with parted eye
When everything seems double.

In other words, they could, for a moment at least, see or experience however dimly, two realities simultaneously. It made me wonder what is real and what is not. Having entered this Virtual World, where I was now riding through the countryside from the city, I felt an affinity with the lovers fleeing into the forest. But in this Virtual World was I attempting to escape from the demands of one mission in favour of another? Or more significantly, was I running away from something in the Real World, which I had left behind?

Like those lovers in the forest, the question I was asking was how real was this Virtual World, in which I too was looking with 'parted eye', at this my new life but also at the life I had left behind at *4 Psychotherapists 4 U.*

Thinking of *A Midsummer Night's Dream* was prompting me to ask, what is it to be awake or asleep; to be in my world and my time and yet in another world and another time? How does a child, a lover, an adventurer, an actor know what is real and what is fantasy? What is it to be oneself? What roles do we play? What pretences do we embrace? Who is it that I really love? Is it Ever, or is there someone else? Is there some other person, hidden within my subconscious, whom I admire, miss and love in the Real World, whilst I am in my Virtual World?

I reigned in my horse and watched the Thames lazily flowing as I started to come to terms with myself. I looked from the river to the countryside around me. Shakespeare, or whoever it was who wrote these plays, was of his time. He or she was mirroring the beauty, not just of people, but of Nature itself, of the wild thyme, musk roses and eglantine where,

….sleeps Titania some time of the night,
Lulled in these flowers with dances and delight.

I wasn't just awakening to challenge my theories about Shakespeare being a marketing ploy, but rather waking to the 'deep down' nature of life itself and my responsibilities within it, both at home and here in my 'dream'. In short, I needed to recognise a love that was within me, for someone to whom I had never professed it.

CHAPTER 30

T hat evening I arrived in the pretty riverside town of Marlow where I saw some newly built houses, which I recognised as quaint picture-card historic buildings that I had seen before in the real world. The inn was comfortable and the food tolerable. I slept well, before setting off, on a different horse, early the next morning on the way to Oxford.

I arrived in the late afternoon, at the tavern on the Corn Market, run by John and Jennet Davenant. It was a homely inn, which the Davenants had recently started to turn into a good business. They had moved from their home near the theatres in Southwark, just a couple of years earlier, because of Jennet's health. They knew Augustine Phillips very well, and were anxious to know what he was doing now.

I was aware of the scandalous story, that Jennet 'knew' William Shakespeare as being more than a good friend. Her son William, to whom Shakespeare was godfather, was to become a great dramatist himself in later years and to claim that his godfather was his biological one. But that William Davenant was not even born when I arrived at the 'Salutation Tavern.' Jennet, however, was pregnant. She had already had a little girl, Jane, and was hopeful that after her problems in London, where she had lost 6 children, she would be able to give birth successfully again to a healthy baby. John and Jennet appeared a happy and contented couple.

I mentioned that I was on my way to Stratford, to visit William Shakespeare. They showed some interest and I noticed that Jennet quickly looked to one of the rooms. John, however, did not take up the topic of Shakespeare as a matter for conversation. He was more interested to hear how I, an alien, had come to London, presumably from the African coast. I made up a tale of a Moroccan father and a Spanish mother, which had some truth in it, except at that time, neither my mother nor father had been born and wouldn't be for nearly 400 years! I tried to get the Davenants to speak of Shakespeare, but they merely said that the Shakespeare they knew was one of the sons of John Shakespeare, who had been a business acquaintance of their father and was a glove maker. I eventually asked outright, whether he was one of the playwrights at the new Globe Theatre. John and Jennet said that they couldn't tell, as the Globe had only been erected at the time when they were making plans to come to Oxford. John then quietly made it clear that I was asking too many questions for a black man wearing the Queen's Colours. I realised that I was being stone-walled. Most of the people staying at the tavern that night ate together, but I noticed that one kept to his room and had his food taken to him. I was so suspicious that I determined to see who he was and planned to arise early to watch his door. But alas, I slept in and never set eyes on him.

I found that the other guests were fascinated by my skin colour and some would 'by accident' touch my hand or my arm. One woman even felt my brow, wondering if I were too hot! To have touched a black man was, apparently, a great adventure to talk about with one's friends.

I set off the following morning, passing close-by, the scorched doors of Balliol College, which had suffered the heat from the executioner's fire that had burned to death Thomas Cranmer, the Archbishop of Canterbury. He had professed the reformed faith in the age of Bloody Queen Mary. Oxford, however, was a city of martyrs, both Protestant and Catholic, depending on the beliefs of the reigning monarch. Although it was a place renowned for its learning, it was one where it was best to keep your mouth shut in matters of religion and politics. Perhaps that was why John Davenant was reluctant to talk to someone wearing the Queen's Colours. Maybe he thought that I was one of the spies engaged by Robert Cecil, Elizabeth's Chief Minister.

I stayed at another pretty village, Shipston-on-Stour, the next night and then I rode onwards towards Stratford the following day, crossing Clopton bridge in mid-afternoon. I immediately went to New Place, a most charming large house, which I understood to be the home of the businessman William Shakespeare. I presented my credentials, but was told that he was not at home. He had left for London two days previously. I quickly asked if he had stayed in the Salutation Tavern in Oxford and was told that he usually did. I enquired if I could meet with his wife, but was informed that she did not receive visitors. The man had the courtesy to read my letter of introduction from Augustine, but with sincere apologies he repeated that Mrs Shakespeare did not talk to visitors on her husband's behalf.

I took lodgings at a local tavern, which was close to a burnt-out building. I asked what the building had been and was informed that it was the remains of a bakery, owned by Hamnet and Judith Sadler, who were friends of Mr Shakespeare, from New Place. I asked where I might find Hamnet, but was told that many people wanted to find him, as the fire had financially ruined him and he had plenty of debtors. The closest I could get to him was by 'eating my bread', which was served to me by a charming lady. I took it that I was asking too many questions again and reluctantly came to the conclusion that my search was at a dead end.

The next day I went to see Holy Trinity Church, looking down over the river on which a bevy of swans had gathered, as if in imitation of the clouds in the sky. I examined some of the gravestones around the church and found one for Hamnet Shakespeare. I surmised that it was the son of William and Anne Shakespeare, brother of Susanna and twin of Judith from New Place Stratford. I read that he was buried on 11th August 1596, aged 11 years.

I turned and looked at the river Avon again, gently flowing past on this glorious autumn day and in contemplating the sadness of that family, whoever they might be. I also wondered where my twin Jackie was and what she might be doing at that moment.

I returned to the tavern, mounted a horse which was already saddled for me, and headed back the way I had come. Had it been a wasted journey? I thought not, I felt confident that someday I would meet the man himself, but only when both he and I were ready.

CHAPTER 31

I n my absence Ever was enjoying Elizabethan London
staying with Augustine's family and working on the
rehearsals of *As You Like It*. The boys were responding and
developing well into their female roles. Ever was so impressed.

Amelia, back at home at *4 Psychotherapists 4 U*, was
thoughtful. She realised that Jackie was accessing her notes and
was clearly preparing to join, unannounced, Ever and me in
our Virtual World. But Amelia had a further problem regarding
Mrs Prenderghast and Mr Smart, which strangely reflected a
difficulty we all shared. Was it that the consulting room had
disappeared from its normal location, or was it that it just
couldn't be seen, and if so why? Whilst neither of the
complainants, Mrs Prenderghast nor Mr Smart could see the
room from the road opposite when they took photographs to
prove that to be the case, the room appeared to be there. How
could Amelia tell them that they were somehow victims of a
hypnotic overspill? It was that which had allowed them, dream-
like, to think that something was not there, when in fact it was. I
had started to realise a similar phenomenon. Even though I was
completely immersed in my Virtual World, sometimes I had a
slight awareness of being at home. Was it just my familiarity

with the consulting room or something else? I had occasional flashes of being home as if the consulting room was triggering something which made me think of being back in the Real World.

Amelia had also realised that the room had become an important element in her experiment, like the set design in a theatrical production. She was puzzled by the fact that although the room had genuinely journeyed with me, moving from one reality to the other within our minds, it could be perceived in both places. She had kept the door to the room locked and it had only been opened the time that I had briefly come back with the Friar. Those back home couldn't see into the room, nor could they tell whether it was there or not. Even from the outside of the building, there was a blur. But that was not the case on the photographs. Mr Smart and Mrs Prenderghast, having raised this in a letter, were due to meet with her. She needed to prove to them that they were suffering from an illusion, or delusion, a mental diversion from reality, in not being able to see the room. This was something for which *4 Psychotherapists 4 U* could easily provide a remedy. Yet how could she do this without admitting that through her and my experiments in Virtual Reality, there had been a hypnotic overspill that had affected Mrs Prenderghast? She had become so emotionally involved with the issue, that it had subsequently also affected the Chief Planning Officer.

But first, Amelia needed to discuss Jackie's overwhelming desire to join Ever and me in Elizabethan London. This, together with the hypnotic overspill, were so confidential that a time had to be chosen when neither Dafydd nor Maddie would be in the building and wouldn't know that the meeting was taking place. A little mischievously, Amelia suggested a time when Jackie would have been reading the confidential files.

In Virtual Reality, Ever was content at Augustine's but a major problem still remained. Spikey, the Practice cat, hadn't been found in either the Virtual World or the Real one. He didn't appear to be in the consulting room. Ever searched our lodging at Wilkins', Augustine's home, and the theatre in case he had followed Ever there. Ever feared the worst and was worried that the cat may have been stranded between the two worlds. Ever asked Augustine for help and another search was mounted, in which Ever was aided by the Phillips family and some of the boy actors. Ever also sent a message that night to Amelia, telling her what had happened. It read: 'Do you know where Spikey is? We searched everywhere, fear for the worst, don't tell Maddie yet, still looking.'

Amelia, bless her, was not an emotional person, but one that used logic to think matters through. She stored it at the back of her mind for the moment, to concentrate on her talk with Jackie, but it kept impinging on her consciousness as if it were something of significance.

Ostensibly, she had led Jackie to believe that their meeting was about the forthcoming visit of Mr Smart and Mrs Prenderghast. She decided, however, when Jackie arrived, to get straight to the point. Over a cup of tea and a drinking chocolate, Amelia asked outright when Jackie was planning to go into the Virtual World to join Ever and me and whether we were party to her plans. Jackie realised that she had been rumbled and went to speak, but as she did so, she broke down in tears. The guilt of her deception of Amelia, together with her longing to be with Ever, were so intense, that it all just spilled out. Amelia, the ultimate professional, listened calmly and intently, before asking,

"And do you think Jackie, that Ever loves you as much as you do Ever?" Jackie, still somewhat tearful, explained that she thought Ever had gone out to Elizabethan London with me from a sense of duty and loyalty to the relationship that Ever and I had enjoyed before my adventure had begun. But whilst I was away, Ever, in that first phase which led to my brief return with the Friar, had expressed love, so great for Jackie, that they both believed their loves to be equal and sincere.

"Yes." She affirmed, "I am confident that Ever loves me and is yearning for me, even though she is with my brother."

Amelia asked her whether she had prepared enough to leave the Real World and if she felt afraid of entering into a different world. Furthermore, what would happen if she didn't find us at first? Amelia admitted that even she wasn't quite sure exactly where either of us might be. Jackie said, with a slightly knowing look, that if she could be sure to arrive in the proximity of the consulting room, she would be safe enough, in the knowledge that we would soon return. She confirmed, that having read Amelia's notes, she would be able to get to the consulting room. She had also planned to dress like me, taking Ever's clothes but wearing mine.

Jackie was worried about how Amelia would cope on her own with Mr Smart and Mrs Prenderghast. Amelia replied that she had an idea which would sort that problem out to everyone's satisfaction. She asked Jackie whether she was sure she was prepared for the experience and she gave her a few more pointers, before agreeing that Jackie could travel that evening. Jackie was delighted.

There was always some danger with this process, especially in the early days. The two of them hugged and said goodbye. Jackie went off to change and when that was done, she was ready. She had learned from Amelia's notes, that she did not need a vehicle of any form to travel, other than her mind. She looked in the mirror and thought that she made a quite handsome man. My sister was all for appearances, just as I admit that I am, but of course, she wasn't me, and never intended to be me. She was her own self, with her own determination, skill, professionalism and love. So it was that her journey began.

Amelia went into the waiting room. An idea had occurred to her which solved two problems. She was the only one able to unlock the door to the consulting room as she had confiscated the key, which she now used to open it. She just looked in.

There was a lovely gust of air, which enveloped her. Lights flickered a little, but she couldn't determine whether they were from the street or the room itself. The room appeared to be there and yet not to be there.

"Spikey" she called, placing a saucer of milk in front of her, in the waiting room. The cat sauntered out of the consulting room and drank the milk. She watched him and stroked him. When he had finished, she picked him up.

"Back you go!" she said, and so the cat went back into the consulting room as if it were going back to his bed, allowing her to shut the door behind him.

"If what has just happened," she thought, had occurred in the Elizabethan age, "I'd have been condemned as a witch, tied to the cucking-stool, and drowned in the river."

It was raining cats and dogs outside as Jackie arrived, having experienced the push pull; pull push and incredible screeching of the final moments of the journey. But there she was, on the stone floor of my consulting room in Elizabethan London. The light was fading, but she knew where, in the consulting room, I always kept candles in case a client was with me during a black-out. She found some and placed them strategically around the room. She then saw how I boiled water and started to make herself some tea. Her plan was to make herself comfortable, until either or both Ever and I returned.

There was a knock at the door. She opened it to find a drenched bedraggled figure outside.

"Jacob," he said theatrically,

"This is I…. Hamlet the Dane."

CHAPTER 32

Dear Jacob

You told me that you were going into the country in search of Shakespeare but I don't know where you are. It worries me as you are separated from Ever who has been in a very strange environment for such a short time. I am also concerned that the incubation period for one of the severest plagues to afflict the times in which you are residing may be about to start.

I have been undertaking some further research about Hamlet. You may be surprised to know we are not the first to attempt to change the ending of the play. Even in Elizabethan times the play had different endings. Whereas today, we normally think that Hamlet's final words are 'the rest is silence', I found that in the first version of the play to be published, they are 'heaven receive my soul.' I wonder why they were changed?

I've also discovered that one of the most famous actors of all time, David Garrick, in the eighteenth century completely changed the ending. He wrote to his friend,

"I have dar'd to alter Hamlet, I have thrown away the gravediggers and all the 5th Act and notwithstanding the Galleries were so fond of them, I have met with more applause than I did at five and twenty – this is a

great revolution in our theatrical history, and for which, 20 years ago, instead of shouts of approbation, I should have had the benches thrown at my head".

It wasn't just David Garrick, but many people through the ages have tried to change it. But despite their attempts, Hamlet has always endured. Do you really think that you are going to do better than all the previous attempts, even with psychotherapy? Is it worth endangering your life with the possibility of plague or disease, or foolish rides into the country? You haven't ridden since you were a boy. I want you back home.
   Amelia

Dear Amelia
   Ever is staying with friends and is happy to be without me! No need to worry. I'm returning from Stratford as there was no luck there. I knew about Garrick before coming out here. The change of Hamlet's dying words is interesting. 'Heaven' places his end in Christian ideology, closing off other interpretations. 'The rest is silence,' is far better. It maintains uncertainty and still allows speculation. My cell phones are starting to play up. There's lots of interference and I keep seeing the cat! I will contact you from Oxford or London.
   Jacob.

Dear Jacob
   Is the cat part of the interference? I believe he is in the consulting room, causing problems with differing senses of reality. Please come back. I'm really worried about you and I miss you.
   Amelia

Dear Amelia
   There is no need to worry. I left Stratford and am now in Oxford at the Salutation Tavern, with Jennet and John Davenant. The cell phones have improved. I'm no wiser from my trip. William Shakespeare is an elusive man! He knows that I want to meet him but he seems to be

deliberately avoiding me. I didn't even meet his wife, Anne. Sadly, I did see the grave of their young son Hamnet.

I have had time to think while I have been riding. You have made this joyous adventure possible for me. My only regret is that I haven't been able to share it with you. I know that you have been anxious about me, but I am coping well. Although people here generally find me strange because of my mixed race and some are reticent to talk to me about Shakespeare, I am enjoying the experience. The horses have been gentle with me.

There is just one thing that troubles me. You say that you are missing me. The distance between us is far too great. I'm missing the two of us talking together, listening to you, being with you.

Jacob

I knew that I wanted to end the message with 'Love Jacob' but felt that it would be too premature. Even as it was, I didn't know whether to press 'send' or not. I did press it and felt a sense of relief.

I thought that I had better include this correspondence in my notes as it was the first time that I started to realise, or at least confess to myself, that I had a problem too, I was missing Amelia.

PART III

CHAPTER 33

After his theatrical salutation, Hamlet, as I was later informed by Jackie, took his usual chair and seeing that water was boiling said that he would welcome a cup of tea thank you very much. Jackie smiled to herself and decided to wait and see if the Prince was perceptive enough to realize that she was not me. She sat opposite the client and waited for him to speak. Hamlet appeared to be lost in thought as he sipped his drink.

"This is lovely tea," he said at last, "but a bit unusual."

"It's always good," she replied. "If you make it while the water is boiling. If you wait just for a moment, it loses the sharpness of the brew. That's why we take the cup to the pot, not the pot to the cup!"

"Ahh," Hamlet replied, "like the secret of boiling eggs." Jackie looked puzzled.

"You remember," Hamlet continued, "you told me to place the eggs in cold water, bring them to the boil and then take them out after 3 minutes, or place them carefully in the water as it is boiling and take them out after 6 minutes. It is all about timing." He paused, "getting it right." He added and thought some more before continuing,

"Like acting. You know. You have to get your timing right, your entries and your exits, your responses and your cues, your pauses and your silences, the movement of your body as you utter your lines." Oblivious to the fact that he wasn't talking to me, he pondered whether the time had come to fulfil his heaven or hell – sent mission. As far as he was concerned, it no longer mattered which it was. He knew that he had to stop prevaricating. Ophelia's death had taught him that you just couldn't tell when you would die. It was only at that point that you'd know if you might go to heaven or not, or whether there was anything more to know. There might just be silence. You wouldn't be able to hear, to speak, to feel, to think. You'd just be without knowledge merely rotting away.

He got up and started pacing as he spoke, going over in his mind matters that he had raised in his discussions with me so that fragments percolated in no clear sequence. Jackie listened carefully, trying to make sense of them: the question of his parentage; the manner of his father's death; Claudius' taking of the crown; his abhorrence of his mother's incest; the players proving the Ghost's accusations to be correct; his killing of Polonius; his treatment of Ophelia.

He wondered about the wisdom of even questioning being or not and at the despair he had shown at not being as sincere in his resolution as the Player King might have been, had he suffered the wrongs, which Claudius had inflicted on him. Turning from the window and facing Jackie he dramatically played out the actor's lines,

> Pyrrhus at Priam drives, in rage strikes wide,
> But with the whiff and wind of his fell sword
> Th'unnerved father falls.

"You see, Jacob," he said earnestly, "that actor knew how to phrase his lines with exquisite timing, matching his features and his voice to a fiction, to a story that had no actual bearing on his own being. It was as if he had become Pyrrhus himself, in his resolution to kill King Priam. I have learnt from him 'a need for roused vengeance', so that like Pyrrhus, who first paused before killing Priam, it is now for me, having hesitated, to 'let my bleeding sword fall' on Claudius. I've decided what I am going to do. When I have killed the King, we will see if time itself has been righted by what has happened or whether more is demanded."

"What do you mean by that?" Jackie asked.

"I mean that 'more' will mean that I will be silenced by my death!"

He revealed that Claudius had made a wager that in a fencing bout with Laertes he, Hamlet, would win by three hits. It was a trap to kill him. When she asked why he should go ahead with it, he laughed and said that Horatio had asked the same question. He gave her a similar answer to the one that he had given to his friend. When it was time for a sparrow to die, it would die. The same was so with him. When it was his time to die, that is when it would be.

"So, you think it is your time?" Jackie asked.

"I do," he answered. "Are you going to try and persuade me that it isn't?"

"No." She replied.

He looked at her quizzically, telling her that he expected a different reply. But she simply said, "How do you know if it is your time or not until it happens?"

"Precisely!" he replied, thanking her. He gave her a bag of money and made to leave.

As he reached the door, he said to her, "I've been puzzling about you. There is something different."

"Different? She questioned.

"Yes," he replied. "But I realise now that foolishly you are not wearing the Queen's Colours."

Jackie didn't know what he was talking about and made up

an excuse saying that they had been damaged when the clothes were laundered.

"You are not safe without them. Take care"

"Thank you," she said, adding, "will you come again?"

"I doubt it," he replied, "Goodbye."

He left the room and went in the direction of the river. Jackie watched as he raised his hand and without turning around, disappeared into the crowd.

Jackie returned to the consulting room and was making tea when Ever arrived.

"Ever!" said Jackie excitedly.

"Jacob," Ever replied sardonically. "So, you are back!"

CHAPTER 34

Mrs Prenderghast and Mr Smart were also drinking tea in the waiting room of the first floor of *4 Psychotherapists 4 U.* Amelia had been informed that this would be the Practice's final meeting with them before the matter was reported to the full planning committee with the recommendation that the consulting room was to be reinstated at the Practice's expense. Amelia was at her most courteous. Dafydd was somewhat nervous and Maddie, who had joined to take a record of the meeting, was a little anxious. She, in fact, had never been quite herself since the disappearance of Spikey.

Mr Smart explained to them that the Planning Department was in a bit of a quandary. Mrs Prenderghast and he could not see the room on the outside of the building. At their last visit, they couldn't see the room either, but one of Dr Angel's colleagues had unexpectedly walked out of it, while wearing strange attire, together with a reverend gentleman who seemed to be in a hurry to use the bathroom.

When the two of them had left the building, they looked up to where the room should have been and still they saw a void. Mr Smart took photographs, but these showed that the room appeared to be in place. So, was the room there or not? In their opinion, it wasn't and they believed that some sort of trick was being played on them.

"There is no trick," Amelia replied. "But I have to tell you that in my professional opinion it appears that you are suffering from a delusion, which we term 'hypnotic transferability'. It may occur with some people - not many - through the stresses and strains of life and can be easily treated. It is best paralleled with claustrophobia or agoraphobia. The cure is a gradual exposure to the delusion, with which *4 Psychotherapists 4 U* could help. Mrs Prenderghast poo-pooed what Amelia had said, denied that she was delusional, dismissing the suggestion as offensive nonsense. Mr Smart conceded that it was hard to believe.

Amelia asked if she might prove what she said to them. They reluctantly agreed.

She began by asking them some questions.

"Did you see the room before you entered the building?"

"No." They both answered firmly.

"Do you see the door to the room now?"

"Yes." They said emphatically.

"Do you believe the room is there?"

"Certainly not!" They exclaimed in unison.

"May I prove to you that it is there?"

Amelia asked them to sit down and turn their chairs so that they could see the door of the consulting room, but at a safe distance away. Even Dafydd and Maddie had no idea what she was doing. She explained that a consultation was taking place in the room, which involved a number of her colleagues, but she would reluctantly interrupt it. She went to the coffee table and poured a saucer of milk, which she placed outside the door of the consulting room. She opened the door and called 'Spikey'. Then she stood back.

Nothing! She called again. Mr Smart and Mrs Prenderghast sighed in exasperation. Dafydd and Maddie held hands. Still, the cat did not appear. Amelia shrugged her shoulders, saying that the cat must be asleep and walked into the room. Voices were heard, which Dafydd and Maddie instantly recognised as belonging to Jackie and Ever. They all heard Amelia clearly say,

"I've just come to find Spikey"

Having found the cat behind one of the cupboards she picked him up and returned to the waiting room, putting him next to his saucer of milk. Maddie screamed, 'Spikey!' and ran to the cat, who merely lifted his tail and turned his back on her. This was time for lapping milk, not petting.

"Now," said Amelia to her perplexed visitors, "we could start treatment today, but I would recommend that having seen the room in use with your own eyes, the condition may just fade away and by Christmas, you should be back to normal. Astounded, they said they would prefer to see whether it might just go away on its own, as she had suggested before they started any treatment. If not, they would make appointments later. Generously, but a little patronisingly Amelia said,

"The Practice would be happy to provide the service at a reduced rate, just for you two."

With that Mrs Prenderghast and Mr Smart left the room and the building.

"How did you….?" Dafydd began.

"Don't ask," replied Amelia, adding, "It was mentally exhausting and a little hairy but at least Spikey is back safe and sound."

Maddie beamed and Amelia suggested that she might like to take Spikey home for the night.

"In fact," she added, "if you want, you can keep Spikey as your own cat, with the compliments and gratitude of the Practice!"

CHAPTER 35

J ackie had already decided that she wasn't going to reveal her true self to anyone until she knew about the current state of the relationship between Ever and myself. After all, she had insisted that Ever should go out to Elizabethan London with me. Had the relationship stood the test of time and returned to the intensity enjoyed before my adventure had started? If so, she would have to accept the reality of the situation. If not …..?

"So, aren't you going to ask me how it is, living at Augustine's?" asked Ever, while drinking the cup of tea.

"Oh yes, of course," replied Jackie, not knowing who on earth Ever was talking about. "What was it like?"

Ever described Augustine's house which had a communal bedroom. This originally had caused some personal alarm, except that Augustine, before I had left for Stratford, had erected a curtain to provide some privacy for his visitor. He, his wife and young son, who turned out to be Harry from the theatre, slept together. They had a few problems with mice, but not with rats.

"So, I told them," said Ever earnestly, "that they needed to be careful of the rats. I said that it was the fleas on them that carried the plague. This had alarmed Augustine and I realised that I needed to take care about what I was saying as I was starting to interfere with history."

It was just at that moment, that the door suddenly opened and someone twice called out, 'Spikey'. Amelia then unexpectedly came in saying,

"I've just come to find Spikey." She found him asleep behind a cupboard. She picked him up and gingerly tiptoed out again, giving them a wave of apology.

Ever and Jackie both looked surprised, but carried on talking, with Ever changing the conversation by asking how the trip to Stratford had gone. Jackie, putting two and two together, reported that it had been a disappointment. She said that the ride had been uneventful and that William Shakespeare was not to be found anywhere. Everyone she had spoken to denied knowledge of him and the people at the house were called Shaftspeare, not Shakespeare.

"Well, that name is close enough," said Ever. "It may have been him. The people here are not particular about getting names right or about spelling them correctly. Did you show them the letter of introduction from Augustine?"

"Of course," Jackie lied, hesitated then continued, "but they denied all knowledge of him."

"How strange, but you must be disappointed." Ever was staring at her. There was something wrong as 'Jacob' looked confused.

Jackie replied, "Well, I am but it is no great matter. I'm more concerned about Hamlet."

"Well, that's a turn up for the books!" Ever remarked with a sneer.

Jackie ignored the retort and explained that Hamlet had been there for a session. Ever became exasperated saying,

"Every day that you were away, Jacob, I have been here expecting Hamlet, but he never turned up. Then, the only time that I was late because of a rehearsal, was the time that you got back here and he arrived."

Jackie shrugged,

"Well, that's the way it goes." She went on to say that Hamlet was resigned to his fate and that professionally there was little to be done to save him.

"Jacob, I can't believe what you are saying," Ever exclaimed. "You are undermining all that you came out here to do. After all your sessions with Hamlet, are you giving him up? You are so fickle! I can tell you that Jackie would never do something like that." Ever then added. "I wish Jackie were here instead of you. I have realised that I love her, not you. There is nothing more for you here. Why don't you go home? Maybe Jackie will come out to stay with me and sort out your mess."

Ever breathed a sigh of relief. Since I had left, Ever had been thinking things through and had already decided to tell me that our relationship was at an end. Now she thought she had done it. Jackie's heart raced for joy, but she decided to keep up the disguise, at least for the time being. Things could become problematic, even tempestuous when I returned. She questioned Ever,

"Is that how you feel? Do you want our relationship to end because of your love for my sister?"

"Yes, I need to be truthful with you Jacob. You were right. Jackie and I did fall in love when you first left the Practice to come to Elizabethan London. I tried to see if it was a temporary infatuation in your absence. But as soon as I came out here with you, I started to miss Jackie so much. I like you, of course, but I wanted to be with her. It is something inside me, gnawing at me. I am happier with a woman rather than a man. I want Jackie as my life partner."

Jackie coolly asked if the love was reciprocated and Ever thought it was but didn't know how Jackie felt now. There had been no correspondence between them.

"I see," Jackie replied. "Matters of love take time to sort

out. Perhaps you should write to Jackie. Meanwhile, what should we do about the sleeping arrangements?"

"I'll stay with Augustine. You go to Wilkins'. He'll be pleased to see you back. You must be tired. I'll walk there with you, as it is on my way anyway."

Jackie was relieved, that she'd have a bed to lie on and that Ever would take her to Wilkins' wherever that was. She said, "We can still be friends, can't we? After all, Jackie is my sister."

Ever remarked on how well I had taken it, but noticed that I had lost my Queen's Colours. That wasn't going to be a problem. The theatre had made a replica for Ever and could make another 'forgery'.

"That's a relief," replied Jackie, picking up a parcel. "I was worried about not having them. Incidentally, it looks as if Amelia has delivered the Elizabethan outfit for you, which Maddie has made. She must have left it when she called in on that peculiar visit a few moments ago, to get the cat!"

"Excellent Jacob," replied Ever, "but her visit was strange. I didn't realise she could come and go like that."

They left the consulting room without Jackie's identity having been detected.

CHAPTER 36

Dear Amelia

I think you should know that Jacob and I are no longer an item. It hasn't worked out. I intend to tell Jackie that I love her and wish to be with her for the rest of my life.

Love Ever.

On reading this, Amelia was confused. She had just received my note from Oxford and I hadn't mentioned anything about Ever and I splitting up, although she had been worried by my sentiments. Was this just a message sent on the bounce, as it were, after me having been jilted by Ever? Was this why I had gone to Stratford? Amelia, usually so calm, felt that she had lost control of the situation, the mission, the team.

She was on her own and wanted to be with me, either in the Real World or the Virtual World. She had sorted the problem with the Planning Department, but she didn't have enough Psychotherapists at the Practice to provide a proper service for the clients. Maybe she should bring in more help from locums and come out to meet me, leaving Dafydd and Maddie to look after the management of the Practice while we were all on a 'staff development course, upgrading our expertise!'

She saw Dafydd and offered to increase his salary on a temporary basis, in order to take charge of the Practice while she was away. He insisted on being made 'Executive Practice Manager' with a permanent upgrade to his salary. She conceded and miraculously his stress levels reduced! She smiled to herself as she started to make preparations to return to Elizabethan England.

CHAPTER 37

As I arrived back in London, I had a mind to go to the Royal Exchange, to buy some trinket or other to make my peace with Ever. It was a fascinating place close to St Helen's Parish, where a Mr Shakespeare from the leather trade used to live, and not far from Cheapside, which was getting a bad reputation for rowdiness.

The Exchange had been founded by Sir Thomas Gresham in the 1560s. The story was that he wanted it as a legacy for himself, as he had no offspring to whom he could leave his wealth. Gresham was delighted that the Queen was going to open it formally. However, much to his dismay, she liked it so much that she wanted it as a legacy for her reign and decided that rather than being named after him, it should be called the Royal Exchange. Money and ambition don't always get you what you want, or that to which you aspire! The merchants and financiers of the new capitalism would do business there and there was also a gallery of small shops. Gresham had since died and the Queen was nearing her end.

Now as I looked at the black and white marbled floors, supporting the great pillars and the images of England's kings and queens, which adorned this monument to Tudor capitalism, everything ironically appeared tired and old, rather like Elizabeth's reign. A sonnet of Shakespeare came to mind,

Not marble nor the gilded monuments
Of princes shall outlive this powerful rhyme,
But you shall shine more bright in these contents
Than unswept stone besmeared with sluttish time.

Maybe the Shakespeare of St Helen's Parish had seen the fading glory of Gresham's edifice.

I tied up my horse and made my way to the galleried shops. I was then waylaid by a group of youths, who couldn't give a damn about the Queen's Colours. They started verbally abusing me, taunting me in racist terms about my colour. It was the first time that I had felt seriously threatened since my arrival in London. I decided against taking my shopping plan any further. I returned to my horse and made my way out of the area, past East Cheap and south towards London Bridge.

I rode the horse to Wilkins' stable and decided to go in search of Ever at the theatre. No-one was there so I made my way back to the consulting room.

There was evidence that someone had been inside, as the cups had been used for tea. I made myself a brew and sat down. It was getting dark. Quite simply I was exhausted and wondering whether I had been totally wrong in my theory about Shakespeare. I fell asleep in the chair with the 'gilded monument' sonnet in my head. I had always had rambling dreams, but the one I had then, I shall never forget. It was of a statue of Hamlet, which I was trying to pull down and destroy. It all merged with what was happening at home before I left it with the Black Lives Matter demonstrations. But what had Hamlet done to me, except show me great courtesy?

I awoke with a jolt, early next morning. Someone was knocking at the door. Blearily and stiffly, I got up from my chair and crossed the room to open it. There stood Augustine.

"Ever said you were back."

"Really?" I replied, wondering how Ever knew.

"So, I came straight away. Will Shakespeare is in town. In fact, he is staying at the Elephant. He wants to see you any time this morning. Must rush as it's the first performance of the Hamlet revival this afternoon."

"Hamlet? Revival?" I queried.

"Well, of course, he answered." "The company is back. It has been a successful tour. Must go."

I felt my world had collapsed around me. Had I been deceived? A revival indeed! It meant that the first performance of the play had already taken place. Hamlet must have died saying the words 'Heaven receive my soul.'

But for me this wasn't the end! I was to meet Shakespeare at the Elephant that very day.

CHAPTER 38

R ichard Wisely greeted me on my arrival at his hostelry.
He told me that Mr Shakespeare was waiting to see
me in the room overlooking the Thames, in which I
had shown an interest a few weeks before.

So, this was the moment I had been waiting for since that
early correspondence I'd had with the man. I was, I must
admit, a little nervous as I mounted the stairs. The door of the
room was slightly ajar. I knocked.

"Come in," he said. I opened the door and saw a figure
standing looking out over the river. He was dressed all in black,
staring into the distance. I was perplexed. I thought I
recognised this man.

"Hamlet?" I questioned.

"No, Jacob," he replied as he turned around, quill in hand.
"My name is William Shakespeare. I'm a playwright and I'd
like you to accompany me this afternoon to a revival of my play
Hamlet at the Globe theatre." I felt faint. He invited me to take a
seat and he gave me a mug of ale since I looked as if I needed
one. Was this really William Shakespeare or was he the Hamlet
to whom I had been giving therapy all this time?

He said that he wanted to thank me for all the help I'd been giving him in the revision of the play. I interrupted him and said that I was at a loss. I didn't know with whom I was conversing. He smiled and said that with a name like Jacob, surely, I would have worked things out! After all, in the Bible, Jacob tried to deceive his blind father by pretending to be his brother Esau. I was blinding myself to a reality in the Virtual World I had entered. I had actually believed that I could converse with a fictional character. He asked me who had been the first Hamlet in his play. I answered,

"Richard Burbage, the principal actor in your company."

"No Jacob," he corrected me. "The first Hamlet in my play was me, whilst I was writing it! I had my sources of course, but I had to create Hamlet in my mind. Just as an actor has to fuse his own personality, his own memories and emotions, conversations and actions, with the role that he plays on stage, so the writer has to do that when he is writing his script, his play. I have to see myself in the role that I am creating from the material I've read. That is how I work. I am my own first protagonist in whatever I write. Maybe, I am not on stage, but I have it up here." He pointed to his head. "In my mind, that is, where the characters first find life. It is there that they start to take on a being of their own but sometimes it doesn't work out quite as I want it to. I have to fashion them, rewrite them and discuss them with people I trust."

"And I was a sounding board?" I asked weakly.

"I'm not sure what you mean by that phrase, but I imagine that it means some kind of echoing back to me of my own words and feelings. Yes, I suppose that is how I used you, once the game had commenced."

"But why did you have to pretend?" I pushed further.

"You gave me the opportunity I needed to be in the role. I could learn from that, from your psychotherapy, what my character was genuinely about."

"Good God, what a fool I am!" I put my face into my

hands, just as, more than once, 'Hamlet' had once done with me. He roared with laughter.

"Jacob, Jacob," he said warmly. "Isn't everything I write a pretence, a dream, a sleep of life itself?"

I had no answer. I should have understood. He was always working, always thinking, always pretending. I asked him what he had learned, and he told me that he had discussed our sessions with Richard Burbage and that between them they had made alterations to the play and to Hamlet's final words 'Heaven receive my soul'. But he stressed that you can't arbitrarily find solutions.

'Plays grow and mature,' he said to me. "A change in the ending of the work comes about through an ongoing acquaintance with its progress and with the growth of its characters. The narrative and the character interact in my mind as I write and in the minds of my actors as they rehearse and even as they perform. It is such a developmental interaction that is needed to determine the final words."

He continued by assuring me that plays are written not only to entertain us but also to entice us to confront our prejudices and expectations and to answer questions about what has been performed in relation to our own experiences. This he termed, holding a 'mirror up to nature.'

In answer to some of my questions, he confirmed that he had played the Ghost in the first performances of *Hamlet*, but now, had so many scripts to write, whilst he felt at the height of his powers, that he needed to give up acting for a while at least.

I established, that he was the writer of the plays, that he did come from Stratford; that he had been in the Salutation Tavern, Oxford on the night that I stayed there on my journey to see him; that unknown to me, his wife Anne had seen me through the window of their house, New Place; that the bread that I had eaten at the tavern in Stratford, had indeed been secretly baked by his dear impoverished friend Hamnet Sadler and served by Hamnet's wife Judith.

I wanted to ask him many other specific questions about his work, his family, the death of his son, his method of writing, and why death and time seemed to haunt him. But time got the better of us.

He excused himself as he wanted to change into his normal clothes. That done in an adjoining room, he returned to me as I stared at the River Thames. He clasped me around the shoulders and suggested that it was time to go to the theatre.

So it was that, with the playwright, I had the privilege of seeing the first revival of *Hamlet, Prince of Denmark* at the Globe. I anxiously awaited the Prince's final words. When they came, it was true to the character within the narrative that I had witnessed. William Shakespeare, my client – my Hamlet – was next to me. As the Prince died, my eyes filled with tears, but my mind still grappled with the confrontations that are the play. I realised that there are no answers, no finalities, no resolutions, only the ambiguous uncertainties, encountered throughout, by the protagonist and encapsulated in the last words he uttered,

'The rest is silence.'

EPILOGUE

After the performance I made my way back to the consulting room and was surprised to find Amelia waiting for me.

"I can tell that you have met him," she said. "Isn't he a wonder?"

"Yes," I answered with tears in my eyes. When she saw them, she embraced me and we kissed for the first time.

xxx xxx xxx

O Time, thou must untangle this, not I
'Tis too hard a knot for me t'untie.

So says Viola in *Twelfth Night*, who, disguised as a young man Caesario, models herself on her 'dead' brother Sebastian and is wooed by the Lady Olivia. It all comes out well in the end, when Sebastian, who was thought to have drowned, turns up and marries Olivia. This allows Viola to admit that she is a woman and marry Duke Orsino, the suitor that Olivia has rejected.

The revelation that she is Viola and not Caesario, comes in the final scene when still in disguise, she meets with her brother in front of Olivia, Orsino and the captain Antonio, who rescued Sebastian from the sea. Antonio, on seeing the twins together, before they had seen each other, asks,

How have you made division of yourself?
An apple cleft in two is not more twin than these two
    creatures.
Which is Sebastian?

Whilst Olivia, in amazement comments,

Most wonderful!

It seems to me that this play, certainly written by William Shakespeare probably in the same year as *Hamlet*, has a particular resonance for Ever and Amelia, Jackie and me. We each had to be aware of our own disguises in order to discover our real selves.

Amelia and I didn't stay at Wilkins' that night but took a room at the Elephant, where the next day Augustine found us with an invitation to a rehearsal of *Twelfth Night*, involving Ever.

I felt apprehensive. I hadn't told Ever I was back, never mind that I had spent the night with Amelia, who told me not to worry as time would sort it out.

We arrived at the theatre where Augustine asked me to read the part of Sebastian in the final scene of the play. I felt honoured to do so. Viola, as Caesario, had her back to me, but I noticed that she was dressed like me. As Olivia said, 'most wonderful', and Viola turned to face me, I saw that it was Jackie. Disciplined, I kept to my script saying,

Do I stand there? I never had a brother,

Nor can there be that deity in my nature
Of here and everywhere. I had a sister,
Whom the blind waves and surges have devoured.
Of charity, what kin are you to me?
What countryman? What name? What parentage?

Jackie answered,

Of Messaline. Sebastian was my father,
Such a Sebastian was my brother too,
Do not embrace me till each circumstance
Of place, time, fortune, do cohere and jump
That I am Viola.

"No, you're not," I said, "But you are my twin sister." With that, in contradiction to the text, I clasped her in my arms.

Ever was playing the role of Orsino and Amelia was standing in for Olivia. No-one had to explain. I realised all that had happened. Amelia had known since before I returned from Oxford that Jackie and Ever were in love and that she and I could also be together.

It is so strange, how the subconscious works and how fiction plays out reality.

Augustine laughed and reminded me that if I was ever in trouble, I could rely on him to put it right!

Amelia and I decided to return to the Practice, but despite concerns about 1603, Jackie and Ever wished to stay on in London for some time longer. In public, Jackie would keep up the pretence of being me. Those in the theatre would concur that what matters was not outward appearances, but what lies beneath - the love of one person for another, irrespective of gender.

So, it is with this story that I have presented to you. Amelia and I are happily living together and working at *4*

Psychotherapists 4 U, which now has branches in various centuries. There is still a consulting room in Elizabethan London, which for the moment at least, is staffed by my sister Jackie, known as Jacob, and Ever.